Two Miles

A Rogue River Tale

ANGELA DARLING

ISBN: 978-0-578-66411-8

DEDICATION

For Olivia.

We carry these wounds with us… but we're never defined by

them.

I miss you.

PROFOUND THANKS

To the amazing people of Rogue River.

You'll be seeing more of me in the very near future, friends.

CONTENTS

"And what rough beast, its hour come 'round at last,

slouches towards Bethlehem to be born?"

~ Yeats

TWO MILES

FOREWORD

I remember walking up to that area for the first time, all of my senses on heightened alert, trying to get a feel for whatever it was that haunted this land.

I walked up to the guide, the shop littered with souvenirs and bumper stickers, and smiled.

I told him I was a novelist and was writing a book about this area.

I told him I was the world's biggest skeptic.

I told him to make me a believer.

The place I'm referring to is the Oregon vortex. A small patch of woods in the Oregon wilderness that has defied explanation for centuries. A small piece of earth that the local Native Americans called "forbidden." Their horses would never want to enter.

And then there was the physics.

The vortex seemed to defy the laws of quantum

physics for decades.

In 1904, it was used as a base hub for a mining company that later dispersed, leaving crooked and sliding buildings in their wake.

In 1930, it became a roadside attraction for its claim that the laws of height and magnetic forces no longer applied.

A geologist moved to the area and was in awe of what he found. A man by the name of John Lister bought land in the area in the early 1900s and spent the rest of his life studying the land from a scientific standpoint.

It was rumored that, towards the end of his life, he remarked that "The world isn't ready to hear the truth," and burned his research notes, dying before he could tell that truth to anyone.

We went on a tour guide group, performing little experiments of our own with yard sticks. Two people of differing heights would stand opposite each other, and then switch spots. There was a pronounced height difference.

I wandered into the gift shop afterwards, not entirely convinced, but not entirely unconvinced either. I got into my car and noticed the quiet. Deep in the Oregon woods, the sounds of the freeways or airplanes overhead, everything is gone. The sounds of the animals in the forest were non-existent; there weren't even any bird songs in the trees. Precisely as the Native Americans had declared. I didn't see any squirrels, any birds, nothing.

But this place, there was something wrong with the land. The silence was almost hampering.

Oppressive.

Most of the people were fascinated by the optical illusions of the place.

But I was more fascinated by its history. Over the centuries, there have been unexplained mysteries, wars raged between local militia and Native Americans, reports of Indian burial grounds emerging during rampant flood waters. There's a magic to this land that is undeniable.

I can't say that I'm a believer.

But I'm definitely no longer a skeptic.

~ Angela Darling

CHAPTER ONE

HENRY

May 1843

He woke up with a start.

The dogs were barking in the dark, snarling and growling at the door.

He fumbled in the darkness for his lantern, quickly running his fingers along the top of the nightstand to find a match. His hands were shaking as he sparked a fire in the belly of the lantern.

This was it. Of that he was certain.

A moment later the small cabin was awash in a dim glow, the light pushing back the sable shadows of the dark. All four of his dogs, sturdy Norwegian elk hounds, were scratching and snarling at the front door.

Henry grabbed the Hawken rifle leaning against the wall and pulled the thin curtain back, staring out into the darkness.

A heavy snow had fallen during the night; the entire floor of the woods was covered in a thick layer of fresh powder.

He couldn't see beyond the darkness to what might have stirred the dogs, but he knew something was out there.

The hairs on his arms stood on end; the same sensation he had felt since first walking into the Rogue River forest.

He wasn't alone.

As if on cue, he heard it.

Footsteps. Crunching in the snow, in the darkness beyond.

Moving towards the cabin.

"Odin! Loki!" Henry called to two of his animals, both of them turning their heads to their master, ears straight up.

Henry reached for the door and swung it open, a blast of cold air hitting him like a knife.

"Go!" Both animals ran out into the darkness, barking and snarling and growling fearlessly into the night. Henry shut the door behind him, rested his back against it, listening to the sounds of his dogs.

He stood there quietly, squeezing his eyes shut, focusing intently on the sounds of his dogs, trying to gauge how far off they were. His rifle, good ole Persephone, rested heavily in his arms.

Suddenly he heard a yelp of pain. A loud, cutting cry that broke the silence of the woods. Another snarl from the second dog, and then nothing.

Silence.

A cold trickle of fear ran down Henry's neck. Both animals, viciously protective, now silent.

Crunch...crunch...crunch...

The footsteps continued. Getting closer and closer to the cabin door.

"Max! Come, boy!" Henry cried, his biggest dog, all fur and muscle, stood alert at hearing his name.

Drool dripped down from his jowls. His teeth were bared before Henry even got the door open. Then he was gone. Out into the freezing cold Oregon night, stirring up a dusting of powder in his wake.

Again, he stood with his back pressed against the door, stroking Persephone with the avid desire of a lover. Listening for Max's barks.

His biggest, most ferocious dog did not disappoint. Henry heard him barking all the way into the thick of the darkness, snarling angrily at something, knowing that as soon as he caught up to it, he would lunge for it and rip it apart.

And then, just as before, one long yowl, a yelp, and then silence.

All except for the...

...*crunch...crunch...crunch...*

...of the snow. And whatever was out there, whatever it was that was strong enough to take down three of his massive dogs, was getting even closer to the cabin.

He turned to Freya, the least vicious in the bunch. His companion for many years. She looked up at him, her eyes big and brown and almost reluctantly accepting what she must do.

Henry knelt down to her, rubbed her behind her ear, the way that she liked.

"Girl," Henry started, the sobs already building in his throat. His hands were shaking in fear, and he could hear the footsteps getting closer and closer.

Despite having much more to say to his best friend, he couldn't find the words. Instead he stood, ran his hand along the cool knob of the door, and turned it, opening the door silently.

His eyes peered around the corner, just briefly, too terrified to see what might be coming out of the shadows, and yet he knew he must look.

It was pitch black in the forest and beyond. Snow was still drifting down in silent harmony, oblivious to the horror that was taking place. The marks of his dogs pawprints in the snow shot a deep pang of sadness to his heart.

Freya gave a small little whimper and then ran out past Henry into the dark. He shut the door behind him again, berating himself for being so terrified. Hating himself for feeling so helpless.

Tears streamed down his cheeks, cold in the chilled air. Freya let out a series of rapid barks, more an actress than a genuine tough dog. That was his girl. Too sweet to hurt a soul. Except those that threatened her master.

Her barked ceased about 100 feet from the door.

No battle cry, no death bark, no sounds of a struggle.

Just silence.

And then the footsteps came again.

Crunch...crunch...crunch....

Henry grabbed a chair and placed it opposite the cabin door. He straddled it and raised his rifle, placing the barrel of it on the back of the chair. Stabilizing it squarely at the door.

His hands were trembling, his breath coming out in front of him in plumes in the cold air. He sat in silence listening to the footsteps approach. Now a few feet away from the door.

They stopped just beyond. He could see a shadow under the crack of the door, big and massive. Nothing happened for a few moments.

Silence filled the night as the snow continued to fall quietly around the cabin.

And then there was one loud, sharp knock on the door. Henry's shaky finger pulled the trigger and shot a round shot through the wooden door. It ripped a large hole through the door of the cabin, exposing the night and the winter scene beyond.

Henry sat there for a moment, wondering if he had hit it. He didn't hear anything aside from the shot itself.

He stood up.

Cautiously, slowly, he opened the cabin door.

April 2015

He stretched out his hand and turned his head against the pillow. His fingertips touched only empty bedsheet. Still warm.

The smell of coffee hinted on the air. He begrudgingly opened his eyes.

She was awake.

John groaned and sat up, throwing his legs over the side of the bed. A quick glance at his alarm clock said it was half past seven.

He pushed aside his Glock and grabbed his wristwatch from the nightstand. He slid it on.

"Helen, why didn't you wake me up, babe?"

He made his way to the kitchen, following the scent of coffee wafting in the air like a dog picking up a trail. He heard something else, soft at first, but growing in volume as he approached.

Music. John leaned against the threshold of the kitchen door, a bemused smile slowly crawling across his sleepy face.

Helen's blonde hair was swept up in a messy bun. She was wearing a white OSU t-shirt and her favorite pair of pinstriped comfy pants, the ones that had a big white paint splotch on the knee, remnants of a house remodel from years ago. She had her back to him, and was dancing around the kitchen slowly, a Hozier song pounding out in the background. Helen was furiously whipping eggs in a ceramic bowl.

John was dying for a cup of coffee. For a plate of those amazing, fluffy scrambled eggs that Helen was in the process of making. But he stood there for a minute longer. Just relishing the moment.

She noticed him first and jumped, giggled. That diminutive giggle that she had.

"Baby, you scared me." One of her hands flew up to her chest, to calm her racing heart. Somehow, she had managed to hold onto the egg bowl.

John just smiled.

"You hungry?" She asked him, getting back to work on beating the eggs.

"Starving." He replied.

"I bet. You worked up quite an appetite last night," she grinned, throwing him a glance.

Helen had this ability to go from damsel-in-distress to seductress with just a flash of her eyes. It was one of the things that attracted him to her from the beginning. She was this beautiful contradiction. A mystery that desperately needed to be solved.

That appealed to his very nature. He was the type that needed answers, craved them. He would drive himself through every possible scenario, every possible answer, before he would let it go. That was likely why he decided to become an officer with Rogue River PD.

John was not a believer in the mystic romanticism of mysteries. Everything had a scientific explanation, a reason for every unsolved incident. He spent hour after hour poring over evidence, somewhere between the border of meticulous and obsessed. John felt those traits were welcome and accepted in the type of field that he had chosen.

This is what Helen did to him. She was this beautiful, walking enigma that he had longed to unravel for the longest time. Being married to her for the last five years had done a lot to solve the mystery that was his wife, but there was always something else. One last little thread that he couldn't quite get a handle on.

It wasn't that he believed she intentionally kept secrets from him. Or was hiding something dark and terrible. It was just in Helen's nature to be beholden only to herself, to play her cards closer to the vest than most.

John never felt like he was getting all of her. That was the best way he could describe it.

Part of him worried that when the mystery was finally fully solved, the mystery of the great Helen Shaw, that maybe his attraction to her would dissipate. It went through his mind every time he looked at her.

As he sat down with her at the table, smiling and sipping his black coffee, staring into her light blue eyes, he hoped that she would never be without her mysteries.

"Hey, what the hell are you doing here?" John said as he walked into the small police station.

Dirk Armacost was sitting in the chair next to the door, waiting impatiently for him to arrive. Dirk stood when John walked in, all towering six feet of him, and began.

"She's up to it again, John. This is the third time this month!"

John sighed and threw his jacket on the back of the chair behind his small desk. He tossed an annoyed look over to Brad Rhodes, a fellow officer whose desk was across the room. He smiled at John. Police Chief Hartley's desk was empty in the corner. He hadn't arrived yet.

"Dirk insisted he speak with you, John." Brad said, a bemused smile across his face as he turned back to his computer screen.

Dirk moved over to the chair across from John's desk. "Third time, John! Something has to be done!"

John groaned softly, folded his hands and looked towards Dirk. "Have you thought about closing your gate, Dirk?"

Dirk scowled. "Why is it my problem? Her dog has gotten out three times in the past month and shit in my yard! Can't you take a report or something?"

John's eyes shot over to Brad briefly, trying to simmer his rising frustration when he saw Brad's concealed smile.

"How about I go over there and talk with her? Will that settle it for you?" John asked.

Dirk brightened. "Hell yes! Next time I see her dog in my yard, I'm taking my gun to it."

John stood and placed a hand on Dirk's back as he led him out of the police station.

"Now, Dirk, that's not a good idea. You know that, buddy. You know that would get you in more trouble than anything else."

Dirk Armacost was a big guy, in his mid-50s, with the mental maturity of a teenager. A big piledriver of a man who was in a work accident a few years prior. John knew he had to dig deep into his reserve of patience and understanding whenever he saw Dirk in his office.

Dirk nodded in reluctant agreement. "Okay, John. Okay."

And then he was gone. John stood for a moment, already deflated by the day, and only looked up to Brad's laughter.

"I'm sorry, buddy. But you know you're his favorite. He wouldn't talk to me." Brad began, the report he was working on momentarily forgotten.

John nodded and grinned. For whatever reason, years ago, Dirk had decided that John was his go-to man. Most of his complaints were relatively harmless. And he was glad that Dirk had a friend in the community that didn't shun him the way most of Rogue River seemed to.

"I guess that maps out my morning," John said, grabbing his jacket and zipping it back up. The early spring air in Rogue River had a bite.

"Anything I should be aware of before I go?"

"Yeah, swing by Porter's Bakery on your way back. Susan called and said they had some vandalism overnight." Brad replied, his eyes already back on the glow of his computer screen.

"Great," John groaned. "And what will you be doing while I'm out there saving the world?"

Brad chuckled and ran a hand through his hair. "I'm catching up on reports from the beginning of the century, John. You know you thrive more on the front lines."

"Front lines of a bakery vandalism and a dog shitting in a yard. This is the riveting stuff I signed up for," he replied sarcastically, a smile working its way across his mouth in spite of himself. "I may need to call for backup."

"Guaranteed. Be safe," Brad replied, and threw him a wave.

The small hamlet of Rogue River sat on bed of the winding river of its namesake. The population hovered around the 2,000 mark and had never grown beyond that as far back as John could remember.

He and Helen had moved to Rogue River a few years ago. Prior to his placement at Rogue River PD, they were living near Portland. She had studied at Oregon State University and moved up to Portland to be closer to friends when they met.

Their romance was a whirlwind; they married about a year after meeting each other. John thought it was partly due to Helen's desire to get out from under the thumb of her parents. They lived about three hours away in Corvallis but, over the years, had proven themselves to be very strict and conservative in their rearing of Helen.

The town slowly trailed by outside the window of his police cruiser, going slowly over the Depot Street bride, the river running angrily beneath him. John figured he would deal with the easiest task first.

He turned onto Star Lane and pulled up to the small bungalow, a mailbox with the name "Armacost" in block letters sitting out near the sidewalk.

John got out and walked across the street to a small duplex. He rapped on the door.

Elizabeth Murdoch answered the door, her hair haggard and unbrushed. She wasn't surprised to see him there, but mild annoyance flashed across her face.

"Again?" She simply asked him.

John nodded.

She stepped aside and motioned for him to come inside. Dexter, her plump Lhasa Apso, yipped over to his feet, his tail wagging in excitement. Even Dexter was familiar enough with John's presence that he got more excited than threatened. John bent down and patted Dex's head. "You're the cause for all of this, aren't you, you little shit?"

Dexter yipped excitedly in reply, and disappeared into the kitchen, following his master.

Elizabeth called out from the kitchen. "Coffee, John?"

"Sure," he replied, standing and moving around the small, cluttered living room. He wandered over to the mantle and his eyes ran over the old framed photographs littering it. Some of the photos were more recent, photos of Elizabeth's immediate family and grandchildren. But then others were much older; rigid, stone-faced looking men, standing tall. Their bodies almost thin and waif-like, and yet he could tell they were strong and hardworking, worn men that had known how to make a living.

There was photo of one man at the end. Black and white, littered yellow with age, worn around the edges of the picture. He was grizzled with leathery skin and a long beard. He probably weighed about 130 soaking wet, but he had sparkling, kind eyes and a bemused smile on his face. He was sitting on a barrel in front of an old cabin. Next to him was a table filled with small animal fur pelts.

Elizabeth came into the room with two coffee cups in hand.

"Black, just like you like it," she said with a smile and handed it over to him.

"Thanks, Beth." He sipped and winced.

Hot and biting.

She knew how to make a good cup.

Beth noticed his gaze at the photo and said, "That was Henry."

She moved to the living room couch and sat down.

"Henry?" He turned to her, questioning.

"My great, great grandfather. He was a fur trapper in this region back in the early 1800s."

John sat down across from her. "I wasn't aware you were from this area. I mean, I know you grew up in Rogue River, but didn't know your family stretched that far back in this region."

Beth smiled, running a hand through her long, gray hair. Dexter jumped up on the couch and curled up beside her. She took a sip of her coffee and glanced up towards the photograph.

"Oh yes, from way back when. That photograph is the last surviving picture of him. It was taken right before he disappeared."

This caught John's interest. "Disappeared?"

She stopped mid-sip and stared up at him. She put her cup down on the chipped coffee table in front of her. "That's right, I keep forgetting you're not a Rogue lifer."

Her gaze drifted once again to the picture on the mantle, her eyes hazy and haunted.

"It wasn't a big deal in those days. I mean, it was the 1840s. He was a mountain man. He had a family to feed and animals to hunt. It wasn't uncommon for men to wander off into the woods for days or even weeks on end. It wasn't until the spring thaw that his wife, my great, great-grandmother, really became worried. I remember the story that I heard growing up. My parents used it as a cautionary tale for us children."

"What was it?" John asked eagerly. Too eagerly.

Beth smiled at him, picked up her coffee cup again. "It was nothing, John. It was just a parent's way of keeping their children under control. They'd often tell us if we didn't behave, we'd disappear just as Henry did. It became the running joke in our family."

"He just disappeared? Without a trace? No trace of him was ever found?"

"Well... not him." Beth said as she put her cup back on the table. One of her hands moved to Dexter's back and pet him reassuringly.

"Henry had these dogs. Four beautiful Norwegian elkhounds that he always brought on his trips into the wilderness. Strong, virile creatures. It wasn't until almost winter that following year that they stumbled across the cabin. And what was left of the dogs."

John leaned forward. "What do you mean, 'what was left of the dogs?'"

A darkness crossed over Beth's features, suddenly lost and trapped in the past, a past that she was only told about in bedtime stories. Of the most macabre variety.

"Something had killed the dogs. Broken their necks. Their bodies lay rotten on the ground underneath the snow that was beginning to fall. The skin on the animals old and dry like paper; brittle, dead. Their heads, well… something strung their heads up on the nearby trees. A stick driven through the skull and into the tree, two heads on either side of the pathway leading up to the cabin. A kind of macabre pack of sentries."

"Jesus. This happened here? In Rogue River?"

"Yes. A little further north of the river. They never found any trace of Henry. All they found was a chair knocked over and a bullet hole in the door. His body was never found."

John sat in silence, turning back to stare at the picture again, as if there was something in his eyes or his face that could explain what happened to him.

He felt that first familiar twinge of the unknown. The unknowable. Mystery. And it bothered him.

"Where up north?" He asked Beth, his eyes intently on hers yet again.

She looked a little taken aback, a little surprised. And then she laughed. Heartily. It rolled from her chest loudly and Dex looked up at her, amused. "You're not going to find anything up there now, John. It's been over 170 years. I doubt you're going to find anything more than what the constables didn't catch."

John stood, challenged, and smiled at her. "Have you met me, Beth?" He threw back the rest of his coffee and sat the empty cup on the table. He moved over to the door.

"Thanks for the coffee, Beth. And keep Dex off Dirk's lawn, okay? He's going to lose it."

Beth smiled. "Of course, John. I will."

"I bet it's that asshole punk kid, Danny Ellis' boy! He rides by here on his bike and throws eggs at the door," Susan screamed when John stopped by. He let a little smug grin slip as he stared at the egg yolk littering the front façade of the bakery. He couldn't help but find the irony in a bakery being egged.

"I'll look into it, Susan. Did this happen overnight?"

"It must have, John. I noticed it when I came in first thing this morning. That Ellis boy has been a pain in my ass for years."

John motioned to the front façade of the store. "How do you know for sure it was the Ellis boy? Do you have a camera up there?" He narrowed his eyes, focused hard.

In the upper, left-hand corner of the store face, underneath the shadow of an eave, was a camera.

Susan smirked. "This isn't my first rodeo, John. I even did the courtesy of double-checking the feed before I called you." She took a long drag from the cigarette in her hand that was quickly burning into a long stream of ash.

"Alright, alright. I take your word for it, Suze. I'll swing by and talk to Danny about his boy, okay? Will that satisfy you?"

Susan nodded. Snubbed her cigarette butt on the pavement. "For now. But if he does it again, so help me, God..."

John chuckled. He held up his hands in self defense and started walking away. "I know, Susan, I know."

He made a quick visit to the Ellis household to talk to Danny about his son, Brandon. A firm warning for the next time. Danny sighed deeply and ran a hand through his peppered hair. He nodded in understanding.

John crawled back into his squad car and drove back to the station, knowing that Brad was likely waiting for him so they could go out and do their nightly rounds.

When he walked into the house, he smelled something burning.

"Helen, you're burning something, babe," he called out to the house, throwing his jacket on the hat rack next to the door. He emptied his pockets, as he always did, onto the console table next to the door, laying his department-issued Glock 22 next to it.

"Babe?" He called again, walking back towards the kitchen.

It was empty.

A thin vein of smoke was beginning to waft around the room and he grabbed a hand towel to pull the casserole out of the oven. He turned it off and saw a note on the refrigerator.

"Honey, went out for

milk. BRB,

H"

He crumpled up the note and threw it in the trash can. John glanced up at the clock.

6:30pm.

He was usually home by 6pm at the latest; Helen probably expected him home at his usual time which is why she left the casserole in the oven while she popped out for some milk.

But the grocery store was a few miles away. She should have been back by now.

John picked through the casserole. The bottom of the pan had begun to blacken, but they should be able to eat most of it. He picked up the phone and called her cell.

It went straight to voicemail. He left a quick message.

"Hey, babe, it's me. Just got home. Wondering where you are. Call me back. Love you."

John grabbed a beer from the refrigerator and threw himself down on the couch in the living room. The news droned on about events happening all over the world: stock market declining, rising gas prices, conflicts overseas.

Nothing in Rogue River. There was never anything happening in Rogue River. John preferred it that way. He played a big fuss up to Brad at the station, but he loved that the biggest issues they had were lawn shitting dogs and punk teenagers.

He woke up to a ringing phone.

Confused, John rubbed his eyes and noticed the TV had long ago automatically turned off. The light outside told him it was well past dusk. He stretched and groaned as he set his feet on the floor, turning on a lamp as he headed into the kitchen.

His eye caught the time on the clock in the kitchen when he picked up the handset.

8:15pm.

"Hello?" He asked groggily, half expecting to hear Helen's voice on the other end.

"Jonathan. Is Helen there?" The voice on the other end of the line was already severe and serious, and he knew that it was Helen's mother.

"Hello, Eleanor."

"Is she there?" His mother in law persisted, ignoring his greeting entirely.

John sat down at the table, wringing the cord on the end of the handset around his fingers. "No, she's not."

"When will she be back, Jonathan?" Her use of his full name always irritated him. She had always kept him at arms' length, speaking to him like a stranger with civilities rather than a son-in-law, a family member. It bothered him. And she knew it bothered him.

"To be honest, Eleanor, I don't know. I just woke up and she's still not back from the store." He looked around to see if something had changed in his surroundings; his eyes scanned the room, looking for her purse, jacket, keys, something.

The kitchen was exactly as it was when he came home. Save for the now cold casserole sitting on the stove.

"Can you have her call me when she comes back?" She asked, already impatient to get off the phone with him.

"Ye…" The dial tone rang out before he could finish his sentence. He looked at the handset in incredulity and slammed it down on the receiver.

"Bitch." He muttered and then looked around the kitchen. It was dark; the blinds remained opened from earlier in the day. Early evening dusk was settling into the nooks and corners of the room.

"Helen?" He called to the house, the first ripple of fear beginning to spread across his body.

Where was she?

This wasn't like her. Helen was always reliable, available, considerate. She would be sure to keep in touch with him, to let him know where she was, when she would be back.

He was beginning to worry.

Without another moment's hesitation, he grabbed his car keys and hopped into his cruiser.

The route to the grocery store was pretty straightforward. Down Lloyellen Drive, a right on Evans Creek and the store was a few miles down. He pulled into the lot, the lampposts alight in the fast encroaching darkness. He drove around the lot in a circle, his eyes peeled, scouring the lot for her car.

There were only four cars in the parking lot; none of them belonged to Helen.

That ripple of fear began tickling the back of his neck even deeper now.

He got out of the car and walked into the store, a small bell announcing his arrival. A cashier on the far end of the fluorescent-lit store was busy stocking candy at a register. She turned when he came in.

It was Mitzy Price, a high school student who worked nights at the Stop 'N Save.

"Hi, Officer Shaw. How are you?" She asked.

"I'm good, Mitzy. I'm good. I was just curious if you saw my wife in here earlier this evening?" His face must have given away his growing concern, because Mitzy's face darkened.

"No, I haven't, Officer Shaw," she began.

"John, please."

"John." She responded.

"How long have you been here tonight?" He asked her, trying to establish a timeline.

"I've been on shift since 4:30pm. All evening. We've been really slow. If she came in, I'm sure I would have seen her."

John nodded, that gnawing, growing fear beginning to permeate every cell in his body. His stomach sank.

"Okay, thank you, Mitzy. I appreciate your help," he replied, making his way back to the Dairy section. As if he might somehow be able to pick up some trail that she came through, that she went to the one place that he knew she might be. The only lead he had in his wife's whereabouts.

The Dairy section was empty, quarts of milk staring at him beyond his reflection in the glass of the untouched doors. He caught a glance at himself in his reflection and was surprised to see how haggard and terrified he looked.

Most people going through something similar would have something to do, someplace to go for help. They would come to him. To help him sort through these probles. Figure out next steps.

He had nowhere to go.

No one to turn to.

The thought was paralyzing to him in that moment. It hit him hard for just a second and, as a deer might stand in the glare of the headlights of a car, he couldn't move. Couldn't think.

He couldn't help but go over every single thing that happened that morning.

Searching for some minute detail, some mediocre clue that he had ignored in passing, but might be able to explain where she had gone.

The night before, they had an amazing night. They connected; it was passionate and intimate. She stared directly into his eyes when they let go together, his face fell into the waves of her blonde hair afterwards, catching his breath, relishing her scent.

The next morning, her silly dancing in the kitchen, the scrambled eggs, coffee, the affectionate teasing. Was there something there? Something he was missing?

Mitzy had walked down the aisle at some point during his reverie. She was staring at him in confusion, horror. John knew she'd likely run to her girlfriends and tell them about the time that Officer Shaw spazzed out in her store.

He waved a quick goodbye and walked out to his cruiser.

What now?

Maybe she left me, he thought and then immediately felt ashamed of himself for giving that thought a moment's residence in his mind. He was man enough to admit that he didn't know everything. But he knew that they were happy. Had been happy. She had been happy.

Hadn't she?

The lingering mystery within his wife; that sprang to his mind right then. Perhaps there was more here than he was allowing himself to believe. Before he knew what he was doing, he was already halfway back to his house.

If she suddenly showed up, he wanted to be there. And yet he knew he needed help.

He needed an objective perspective.

On his way, he called Brad.

CHAPTER TWO

ROGUE RIVER

He stretched out his hand and turned his head against the pillow. His fingertips touched only empty bedsheet. Cold.

He sat up immediately, staring around the darkened bedroom, the shades drawn, blocking out the early morning dawn attempting to peek into the room. All at once the previous evening flooded him with haphazard memories, and he felt that urgent pang of sadness rising up in him yet again.

He sat up, put his head in his hands, and felt the well of tears that he had been pushing back and pushing back begin to overcome him. John sobbed softly into his hands, flashes from the night before still running through his head.

Brad had come over quickly, concern written all over his face. Brad, his wife and the Shaws had often invited each other over for weekend dinners. Brad knew Helen.

When he saw John open the door, he was shocked at his appearance. Usually put together, organized, regimented John Shaw was now haggard and worn down, tired and concerned.

Together they sat down and brainstormed, as they had numerous times before, going over all of the possible and plausible scenarios in their head. As difficult a task as it was for John to do, he knew it had to be done.

"Brad, she didn't make it to the store. She didn't make it a few miles down to the store. Where could she have gone? She wouldn't have left me. She was happy. We... we were happy." John said, just as the phone rang.

He jumped up quickly, knocking the kitchen chair back. It fell to the linoleum in a clatters. John grabbed the phone, noting it was now almost 9:30pm.

"Jonathan." Eleanor's voice again, and this time John broke down. Deep, wretched sobs came pouring out of him, surprising Brad and likely Eleanor. The line had gone completely quiet. Out of the corner of his eye, John could see Brad hang his head. The cold casserole still sat half-burned on the stove, unloved.

Then, after a moment, softer this time, "Jonathan?"

"Yes, Eleanor." His voice was breaking. He was struggling to keep it together.

Quietly, as meekly as he had ever heard her before, Eleanor asked, "Jonathan, where's my daughter?" Her voice was shaking as well.

"I… I don't know, Eleanor. She's disappeared."

"What? What do you mean, 'she's disappeared?'" The meekness was gone. In its place was alarm. And a lot of anger.

"I came home from work and she was gone. She left a note saying she went out for milk and she never came back." His voice was slowly growing in strength. As big a leaden feeling as it gave the pit of his stomach, saying the words seemed to relieve him somewhat. He was bringing Brad and Eleanor into this. He was going to have help to find her. That washed a little relief over him.

"Well, go and fucking find her!" Eleanor screamed, her meekness all but a memory.

Her screams were so loud John had to pull the phone away from his ear. Brad noticed and winced.

"We're trying, Eleanor."

"Trying has the intention to fail. Just fucking do it! Isn't that what you do? Isn't that what you guys moved all the way over there to do?"

Eleanor was furious, her anger coming out in vitriol waves. It wasn't anything he hadn't seen before. Usually it wasn't directed at him. It was usually directed at poor Helen.

But John had seen the conniving ways she had of being manipulative. In truth, it was likely one of the reasons why Helen was so excited about moving to Rogue River in the first place.

To marry him.

To escape her family.

And then a cold rivulet of fear trickled down his spine. Maybe that's why she left. Maybe she wasn't happy. Maybe she only married him to escape her abusive family.

"I mean, you're an officer of the law, are you not? A detective? Aren't you supposed to go out there and follow leads? Find clues? Interrogate suspects? DO SOMETHING other than sit on the other side of this phone call whining like a baby?!"

"Eleanor…"

"I mean it, Jonathan. You need to find her. You need to go now and find her. Do you understand me? Do you unders…"

"Eleanor, we're doing all we can right now…"

"That's fucking garbage, Jonathan. You're sitting in your kitchen right now, aren't you? I called you on the house line. I bet that's exactly where you're at. Which means you're not out finding her! Track her car! Check her credit card transactions! DO. SOMETHING!"

"Eleanor, truly, we're following every lead we can right now. The only thing we had going for us at this point is the fact that we know she was heading to the store. But she never made it."

"So, go scour the fucking woods! I mean it, get out there! If Daniel went missing, I would not leave a stone unturned on this planet until I found him!"

In the most inappropriate of moments, the most inopportune of reactions, John smiled. The image of Eleanor as a 26-foot Godzilla monster wandering through the city to find her poor, diminished husband cowering under a rock, trying to hide from her made him laugh. He couldn't help himself.

Eleanor heard.

"Are you fucking laughing right now? Are you seriously fucking laughing right now, Jonathan? What in the hell is so goddamn funny?! Helen is missing! Don't you care?!"

"Of course, I care, Eleanor. I'm sorry. I just don't know how I'm supposed to react in this situation. I didn't mean to disrespect you," he said, rolling his eyes in Brad's direction.

Brad managed a wan smile.

"Then act like it! Get out there! Daniel and I are driving up. We'll be there tomorrow afternoon. Time is precious in situations like this, as I'm sure you well know. And I can't rely on you to do your fucking job. We'll be there by 3!"

And without a goodbye, she hung up.

John stood with the earpiece up to his cheek for a moment and then slowly hung it up.

"Well, that went better than I thought it would," John replied, an exhausted smile creasing his lips.

"She's upset. She has a right to be. But, so do you. She's not the only one suffering. I'll be happy to remind her of that fact when she gets here," Brad began. John waved him off.

"I can handle Eleanor." He replied.

"You sure? She sounds like a nightmare." Brad countered.

"Like you said, she has a right to be upset. If she's here to at least even stay at the house while I go out and scour the woods, track any leads I need to, that would be a help. I want someone here if Helen should wander through the front door…" He stopped for a moment.

Took a deep breath. Swallowed down a lump that was threatening to creep up his throat.

He felt like this was all a terrible nightmare. Just this morning she was dancing around like a lunatic in her kitchen. And now, nothing.

He ran over to the trash can, threw the lid up and started rummaging through the garbage.

"John, what are you doing?" Brad asked.

"Her note. I threw her note away," he said as he found it, mixed in with some cold coffee grounds. Wet, dirty but still intact.

"'Honey, went out for milk. Be right back. Helen.' This is what she left me." He handed it over to Brad, who studied it with a furrowed brow, turning it over in his fingers.

"Did she leave you notes like this often?" Brad asked.

"Yeah, all the time. But she always came back when she said she would. This isn't like her, Brad. I think something terrible might have happened," John replied, almost collapsing in the kitchen chair.

Brad stood up and moved over to him. "Okay, we don't have any other leads other than where she might have been going and when. You are exhausted, John. You need to be here in case she comes back.

I'll go out and drive around, see if I can spot her Jeep in town. See if I can spot any tracks into the woods, anyplace she might have driven. We'll find her, John. We will." He was too tired to argue.

Halfway out the door, Brad turned back. John shook his hand and said, "Thank you. Truly."

He planned on waiting up for her, waiting for Brad to return and give him an update. John didn't realize that he had fallen asleep until he woke up in his bed early the next morning.

Sat up quickly, checking the clock. It wasn't even 6am. The dawn had slowly begun to creep beneath his curtains, letting in a soft light. He followed it with his eyes, let them drift across the room to the empty bed next to him.

John sat up, fighting off those sobs, rubbing his eyes awake. What little sleep he got wasn't great. He actually woke up feeling worse, even more exhausted. But he had to get out there. He had to start combing the roads, combing the streets, get into the right mindset to find some clues and figure out what happened.

John checked his cell phone. Saw a few messages from Brad. The summary was that he hadn't found anything. No trace of her Jeep, nothing amiss in the nearby woods. She was just...gone.

Out of a desperate hope, he called her cell phone again. Again, it went straight to voicemail.

He left one: "Baby, I'm so worried. Whatever it is, we can work it out. We can talk through it. Please, call me back. At least let me know that you're safe. That you're okay."

John left a scribbled note on the counter: *"Baby, if you come back before me, please stay here. And call me. I'll be back soon. J"*

He drove around town despondently. All the usual haunts, be them ever so few, were empty of her Jeep parked out front. He started going door to door to the businesses in Rogue River, their wedding picture clasped in his hand.

It was almost 3 o'clock. Eleanor and Daniel were about ready to arrive, and that was another storm he knew he was going to have to weather. He stopped at the gas station off of the Pacific Highway. One last place before he headed for home. Finally, he got a nibble.

Evan Abney, a pimple-faced college kid, was behind the counter, looking bored while reading a magazine. It was slow and there were only a few customers in the store. He looked up, surprised, when John walked up.

The whole town knew who John was. But he was wearing jeans and a t-shirt, not his badge and gunbelt. It was a little disorienting for him.

"Hi Officer Shaw," he greeted, putting his magazine aside and offering a weak smile.

"Hi Evan. I'm curious if you happened to see my wife drive by here yesterday? Or maybe she came in?" He put down the wedding picture on the counter and Evan laughed.

"I know what Helen looks like, sir. And yes, she did come by yesterday."

John's head perked up. Suddenly his exhaustion was gone.

"She did? When? What time, Evan?"

"Um, I think it was around 5:30 or so. I didn't talk to her or anything. She just paid at the pump, gassed up and then she was gone."

"Where? What direction did she go, Evan? Please, this is very important?" John's urgency made Evan's eyes darken, his eyebrows furrow.

"Is everything okay, Officer Shaw? Are you okay?" Evan asked, concern shadowing his face.

"Please! Tell me, Evan. It's important. Which direction did she go?"

"She went east, sir. East on the Pacific Highway."

John sighed, grinned. Thankful. "Thank you, Evan, thank you. Is there anything else suspicious about Mrs. Shaw that stood out to you yesterday? Was she with anyone?"

The last question caught Evan off guard, but he nodded politely and replied, "No, she was alone. At least it didn't look like anyone else was in the Jeep when she pulled in. But she was…"

"What? She was what?" John asked, the vigor of his urgency surprising even him.

"She was acting a little strange, I guess. I've met her a few times before and she's always been really nice to me. But yesterday she seemed kind of nervous. I don't know… distracted somehow."

John's mind flashed with the thought he had ruminated on the day that she went missing. That mystery. The thing that he secretly prayed he might never solve out of fear of losing her.

Maybe she really was hiding something…

"Distracted how?" He asked Evan, who shot a look to a couple of customers that approached him at the register.

Now it was Evan's turn to look distracted. "I don't know, sir. It looked like she might have been scared. She didn't look at me or say anything to me; she didn't come in at all. And then headed east. I don't know much more than that, Officer Shaw."

"Thank you, Evan. I appreciate your help," he muttered as he turned and walked out the door.

He already had an idea.

John jumped in his cruiser, throwing a glance at the clock on the dash. 2:43.

Eleanor and Daniel would be arriving at the house any minute. But he couldn't worry about that now. He didn't care about that now.

He had to follow this lead.

What was she doing out here? What was wrong? Why did she look strange? Where was she going?

All of these questions swirled around deliriously inside his brain. But he finally knew of one place where he could start.

One place he could pick up the trail.

He pulled up to Porter's Bakery and turned off the cruiser.

John didn't realize how badly his hands were shaking until he sat there for a moment, trying to gather himself. He almost felt like this was all incredibly surreal. The last few days, Helen going missing. None of it seemed real.

And yet he knew the moment he turned onto Lloyellen Drive, pulled into his driveway and saw Eleanor's car parked out front, that she would make this very, very real. A feeling of dread washed over him and he got out of the car.

Susan was mopping the floor when he walked in.

"Hey, John! Did you have a talk with that Ellis boy?"

"Yes, Susan, he won't be bothering you anymore. Listen, I actually came for another reason."

She looked up at him in confusion. Stopped mopping.

"Oh?"

"Do you happen to have feed from yesterday? From your camera out front?"

Her eyes narrowed. "Yes, I should. It automatically records but all video is deleted after about a week. Why do you ask?"

John sighed, thankful he came in today. Fuck Eleanor.

"Can I have a look at it?"

Susan chuckled softly, leaning her mop against the wall. She motioned for him to follow her to the back. Down a short corridor and into a small back room, with a cluttered desk in one corner and a monitor hanging on the wall above their heads. Susan bent over to a small machine next to the desk.

"Do you have a specific time that you wanted to look at it or just review the whole day?" She asked.

"Can you cycle it to 5pm yesterday? And just play it from there?"

"Sure, John," she chuckled again. "Anything specific we should be looking for?"

"My wife's Jeep."

Susan shot him an odd look over her shoulder and then went to work cycling the video to the right point. She hit play.

The feed began to play at regular speed.

"Everything okay, John?" She asked, watching the playback with him.

"I hope so, Susan. She disappeared yesterday. I have no idea where she went." His gaze was focused on the grainy feed, waiting to see her black Jeep drive by.

He could feel Susan shift beside him, sigh deeply. "Jesus, I'm sorry."

They watched the rest of the playback in silence.

"Wait a second! I think I saw it; can you rewind it really quick?" John said.

Susan bent back down, wound the recording back, played it again, slower this time, frame by frame.

The timestamp on the monitor said 5:27pm. Out of the corner of the screen, on the street, he saw the top and side of a black vehicle. Moving slowly through the feed, he confirmed it.

It was indeed her Jeep.

"Where are you going, baby? Where were you going?" He said out loud. Susan shifted uncomfortably beside him.

Another idea sparked in his mind. He turned to leave.

"Susan, thank you so much. I really appreciate your help."

"Sure, John," she said as she followed him out, a concerned look on her face. "I hope you find her. I hope it all works out for you, John, I do."

John nodded in return and opened his cruiser door.

"I do, too."

He walked into the station, surprised to see Police Chief Hartley at his desk. He was often out in the field, hardly ever in the station. But today, John could tell, he had some special attention coming his way.

Hartley stood and made his way over to John.

"I've heard. And I want you to know that I have Brad out scouring the streets yet again. We're going to find her, John." He smiled lightly, one of his hands resting on John's shoulder.

"Thanks, Don. That means a lot. It truly does." He moved to his desk, sat down, booted up his computer.

"Truth is, I have a couple of leads. Evan Abney at the gas station claims he saw her gassing up her Jeep around 5:30 yesterday evening. Said she headed east. Susan's bakery cameras confirm his story. I have one more thing I wanted to check."

He plugged in his username and password and went straight to an internet browser.

Don leaned over him. "East, you say? Towards Gold Hill?"

"Yeah."

"Great, I'll radio Brad and have him head over in that direction," he said as he walked over to the two-way radio on his desk.

Helen paid all of the household bills online. Including their cellular phones.

On a hunch, he logged into his provider's website. Entered the username and password he thought Helen might have used.

Success. He was in.

He navigated the page for quite a while before he found what he was looking for. Her cell phone usage yesterday.

In her history, there were a lot of calls between her and John, Eleanor, Daniel, and a couple of girlfriends she had that she met in Rogue River. But there was one call that jumped out at him.

It wasn't even a number. Just a bunch of zeros where the number should have been. It was labeled, "Unknown." And the call came in at 5:24pm yesterday evening.

"Don, look at this." He called the chief over, pointed to the line on the phone bill.

Don's eyes narrowed suspiciously. "Who the hell was that?"

"I don't know. Any way the cell company can dig into this a bit deeper? Be able to give me a phone number for this call?"

Don shook his head morosely. "I don't think so, Bud. I don't think they're quite that sophisticated, but I can reach out them. Give it a shot."

"That'd be great, yeah." He replied.

"You need to go home. Seriously. Get some sleep, John, you look like a fucking mess. Brad's heading to Gold Hill and I'll see what I can find out about this phone number. We've got it under control."

John sighed. For the first time since she disappeared, he felt like he truly was able to take a deep breath. He had something to bring back with him to his inevitable confrontation with Eleanor. Though he knew it wouldn't satisfy her, at least there were some leads. There was motion. Something was happening.

He stood up and gave Don a hug.

Don, a big, meaty tall guy, wrapped his arm around John's shoulders. "It's all good, brother. We've got this. Just get your ass home, okay?"

John nodded and walked outside to his cruiser.

With a twist of his key, it growled to life. He began the short jaunt to Lloyellen Drive and to Eleanor.

John could tell she was already fuming when he pulled up. The dash clock read 3:44. He sighed.

"Where in the fuck have you been?!" She growled at him before he had a chance to get out of the car.

"I've been out following some leads, Eleanor. Daniel," he said, nodding in his father in law's direction. He nodded back.

"Well, we've been waiting here for almost an hour. Freezing our asses off. I need to hear everything," she replied, walking up the pathway to the front door.

Five minutes later, they were all gathered in the living room, and he was retelling the sequence of events. He also discussed the leads that the team was investigating.

Eleanor stared at him silently, icily. She waited until he was done speaking before she stood, began to pace the floor.

Daniel lowered his head, his eyes tracing the swirls in the design on the carpet below him. Not knowing what to say.

Eleanor moved over to the window. The gauzy drapes drawn but the late afternoon gray sky cast a dim light into the room. She stood at the window, staring out, deep in thought.

Finally, she spoke. "There are only two scenarios here, Jonathan. Either she ran off with another man. Or she's dead."

The cool way in which she said those words chilled John, though she was saying exactly what had been in his mind. She turned suddenly to him, that brash look on her face was back.

"And we both know Helen's no cheater." Her eyes shot lightning bolts across the room at him, but her face fell fast. Crumpled.

The regal, stoic Eleanor Hassek was unraveling before his eyes.

She sat down next to Daniel on the couch, her hand lacing through his. "Jonathan. Just bring her home. Please."

The vulnerability in Eleanor was both jarring and heartbreaking. John had to lower his head. He couldn't look at her.

She persisted. "Please, Jonathan. Promise me. Promise you'll bring her home." Pleading with him.

Finally, he lifted his head. It took all of his strength to respond to her. But he didn't want to tell her what she wanted to hear. He knew it would be a lie. He wanted to be honest with her.

"I will try, Eleanor."

The vulnerability fell from her face, swept out from under her demeanor like a rug being pulled. The vitriol was back. Aimed in his direction.

She stood, towering over him.

"Not. Fucking. Good. Enough." She replied, and with a quick turn on her heels, she was out the front door.

TWO MILES

CHAPTER THREE

LATGAWA

February 2019

He yawned and his arm stretched out, the bed empty beside him yet again. Cold.

John opened his eyes.

Glanced around the familiar bedroom, now devoid of her clothing, her makeup, her shoes. It took him several years to be able to get rid of her things. A part of him always thought she might walk through the door one day. And, as angry as he would be at her for disappearing the way she did, without a word, without a clue as to where she went, he knew that if she walked through the door, he would swallow her up in his arms, kiss her deeply, and whisper in her ear that all is forgiven. That nothing is too big for them to overcome together.

The day he packed up her clothing, he sobbed like a baby.

It wasn't the act of packing up her things. It was what it meant to him.

If he was packing up her belongings, he no longer thought her disappearing was voluntary. That she didn't leave of her own free will. That she would never walk through the door again.

And was most likely dead.

Eleanor still blamed him. She was resolute in her assumption that there was some marital turbulence that Helen had to run away from. The years following Helen's disappearance were nasty. Bitter. The accusations that she flung his direction were not just untrue, but they were extremely hurtful.

He had somehow managed to avoid Eleanor's ire for several years before Helen's disappearance. Eleanor never approved of the marriage and was not shy about making it known. But most of her vitriol was directed at her daughter.

John was counting down the days until she tried to file a lawsuit against him for wrongful death. Of a missing woman. Whose body has yet to be found.

The police force was the only thing that kept him centered, focused. Researching other cases, focusing his attention on other people, other incidents; it helped him contribute and made him feel like his life was worth something. Brad and Don tried, to their immense credit, but every lead turned up dry. After she disappeared, it cast his entire world on its side. He began to question the importance of a lot of things. His work, his friends, his life.

Nothing seemed as important as her.

And he feared nothing ever would again.

Brad was supportive, helping out when he needed to take some extra time off of work. Brad's wife sent over some hot dishes though he didn't have much of an appetite these days. Don was generous in granting him paid leave.

But John never told them about the trips he would take to Gold Hill. The small town lay east of Rogue River, the direction that she had gone that day. No amount of detective work could uncover her tracks in that town. He went around, combing the businesses in the area like he'd done in Rogue River, but no one remembered seeing her.

Most nights he would drive out to Gold Hill and sat at the bar at the Lucky Strike Saloon, twirling a whiskey cup in his hand. Sipping on the whiskey until the ice had finally melted away.

He had no place to be.

One evening in February, he left work, changed clothes and drove out to Gold Hill. He and the bartender at the Lucky Strike were already on a first name basis.

The saloon was dimly lit, the incandescence of fluorescent pinks and blues of the signs in the window breaking apart the dark. A man behind the counter saw him coming and went to work pouring a glass of whiskey.

"Hey, Phil. How are you tonight?" John asked, sitting down at his favorite stool. There were a handful of patrons in the bar: a couple of guys throwing darts in the corner; a woman standing indecisively at the jukebox.

There was a tall, shadowy figure sitting at the far end of the bar, almost obscured entirely by the dark.

Phil tossed the drink down in front of him with a smile. "Thanks, bud." He replied.

John took a sip, relishing the hot warmth filling his belly, running smoothly down his throat. He jumped a bit when he saw the shadowy figure at the end of the bar stood up and began to move.

Phil noticed and laughed. "That's just George. He's basically a piledriver, that guy, but he's a good man."

John smiled wanly, his eyes moving back down to the end of the bar. The figure stood up fully from the bar stool and he was amazed at how tall he was. In the dark, he estimated the man was about 6'4".

This guy wasn't a piledriver. He was a monster.

The glare of the red and pink fluorescent lights washed over his face and he could pick out strong features. Light brown Native American skin, a regal nose, a strong chin. His hair was long, one side was swept up in a few braids.

"Is this seat taken?" He asked when he finally made it over to John, his voice surprisingly soft.

"No, go ahead," John replied, motioning for him to sit.

The man was quiet for a moment, twirling his beer bottle around with his long fingers. Picking the label off the brew one swipe at a time.

Finally, he spoke.

"You know, I know you."

John turned to him, his gaze narrowing. "How could you possibly know me? I've never met you before in my life."

"I keep up on the news around here. I've been following your wife's case for years."

With that, his gaze snapped back in the man's direction.

"I'm sorry, let me introduce myself. My name is Tall Trees. But most people call me George." He reached out a huge hand to John and waited for him to shake it.

"John," he shook George's hand firmly. Smiling.

There was a kindness in the man's eyes that he immediately trusted.

"Tall Trees, eh?" John asked as he shot a smirk over in his direction.

"No idea why they call me that," George replied sarcastically, grinning. He peeled a little more of the label from his bottle.

"You said you followed my wife's case?"

George nodded in the darkness, silent. "You hear the wife of a local cop goes missing, it tends to catch your attention."

John nodded softly, taking another sip of his whiskey.

Instant warmth.

"You must have formulated some theory, some opinion about what happened?"

George nodded again, quiet. He murmured, "Maybe we should go grab a table, away from the jukebox speakers. I have much to tell you."

July 1988

Port Townsend, Washington

He woke up with a start as a firework, a large mortar, exploded right outside his bedroom window. His room was awash briefly in a wave of pinks and purples and then darkness descended once again.

It wasn't just the firework that pulled him from his sleep. John could hear voices, muffled and indistinct. Coming from downstairs.

He glanced at his He-Man alarm clock.

12:08am.

It was the Fourth of July and it wasn't uncommon for people to light off fireworks into all hours of the night, especially given the late dusk time in the summer months. Living in Washington, he'd see booths set up all along the highways, selling snakes and sparklers and missiles and firecrackers. The reservations would often have the good stuff. The M-80s and the mortars.

It wasn't uncommon to hear the fireworks, even this late, but it was strange to hear voices coming from the landing below.

His mother, crying softly. He could tell they were trying to keep their voices down. But there was an urgency in his parents' voices that caused the hairs to prickle on the back of his neck.

Something was very wrong here.

There was a tall policeman taking down notes on a pad of paper. A shorter policeman stood at his side, asking the questions in a hushed voice. From the upstairs landing, between the poles on the railing, he crouched down and watched. Listened.

There was a picture in the tall cop's hand. It was of his sister Jenny. A picture she had taken at the park just a few weeks ago.

John's blood ran cold. Any tiredness and grogginess he had waking up was gone.

"When did she say she would be back, ma'am?" The short cop asked his mother. Diane wiped her nose briefly, muffled another sob, and then answered back quietly, "She said she would be back by 10pm."

The officers gave each other a passing glance, and then the shorter one continued.

"And where did she say she was going?"

"She said she was going to the pier to watch some fireworks with her friends."

The tall cop furiously scribbled on his note pad, taking the picture of his sister and holding onto it.

"And have you tried to contact any of her friends? The kids she was going to watch fireworks with tonight?"

Diane choked back tears. "Yes. I called her best friend Mary, and she said that Jenny had taken off for home around 9 o'clock."

John's father, Alan, placed one hand on his wife's back, trying to support and steady her. He was quiet, his head turned down silently, staring at the floor. It looked like he was struggling to stay on his feet as well.

John's heart dropped.

Jenny was missing? He had just seen her that afternoon, wearing her flowery yellow summer dress. Her hair pinned up on the side. A little mascara framing her brown eyes, some gloss on her lips. John suspected that there was a boy she had a crush on when she went to join her friends at the pier. Someone she wanted to impress.

Mary was her best friend in junior high school. They spent every spare minute together they could. Mary often came over to the house for their spaghetti dinners. She loved pasta, especially the way that Alan made it. She was like part of the family.

That's why John found it hard to not believe her when she said that Jenny walked away from the pier at 9 o'clock. And disappeared.

The tall cop flipped his notebook closed, put the picture in his pocket and nodded over to the shorter officer.

The short officer, a man named McIntosh, spoke again to his

mother. "Mrs. Shaw, it's only been a few hours since she was due back home. Since she's a minor, we can go ahead and put out an APB on a girl matching her description. See what turns up. In the meantime, stay close to the phone, close to home should she wander in."

In that moment John knew that their lives would be forever altered, forever changed in some deep way.

Jenny had disappeared. Reliable Jenny.

She was always on time coming home from friends' houses. She never broke curfew. Never snuck out at night.

John knew something had happened.

And he was infuriated that the cops didn't immediately hop in their cruisers and go out and scour the roads leading back from the pier. The they didn't seem to have any true urgency around it at all. John knew the first few hours were paramount. Their best chance at getting her back.

But they walked out the door, business as usual, leaving his parents to crumple to their feet, sobbing into each other's arms. They glanced up and saw him there, cowering quietly behind the railing, his big eyes staring down in confusion.

Diane called out to him, "Johnny, baby, come down here. We have something to tell you."

February 2019

Gold Hill, Oregon

George motioned for him to slide into a small, wooden booth at the end of the bar, further away and quieter. Though they could still hear the sounds of The Eagles crooning out a familiar tune, but it was diluted. Softer.

George met his gaze, motioned to the whiskey glass sitting in front of him.

"You're going to want to drink that. Toss it back."

His tone was dark, foreboding. The friendly, jovial stranger he had met at the bar a few moments ago was gone. There was an air about him that seemed haunted. Like his eyes held a well of mystery.

Immediately, John was drawn in. Without a word, he did as he was bid and threw back the rest of the whiskey.

Felt the heat traveling slowly down his body. He sighed.

Finally, George spoke.

"How much do you know about this area?" He asked John.

John shrugged his shoulders lightly, feeling the power of the whiskey beginning to work its magic. "I know a little bit about the history. Used to be a lot of Native Americans in the area." He nodded to George respectfully. "I also know there was a fair amount of mining here. Why do you ask?"

George ripped the last piece of label off of his beer, the beer itself had grown warm and piss-tasting. He drank it anyway.

"There's something else. The woods. They're...wrong."

John grinned bemusedly. Shook his head.

"What do you mean, 'wrong?'"

George sighed. "Look, you can take all of this as Indian superstition, folklore. Take it for what I'm offering. Believe it, don't believe it, it's entirely up to you."

John waited for him to continue. Nodded. "Go ahead."

"Your wife isn't the first person to disappear in Rogue River."

John's blood ran cold. He stared at George for a moment, processing what he was saying. He shook his head incredulously.

"I'm on the force, George. If there were missing people popping up in Rogue River, I'd know about it." John replied, already looking for a way to back away from the conversation.

"Today, yes. Today, you would know. But the history, John. The history of this place is what I'm talking about. The world that came before. Before you and I were here."

John shook his head again, the whiskey making him lightheaded and having a difficult time processing what George was trying to tell him.

"So, you're saying that there are missing people from way back in this town's history?"

"That's exactly what I'm saying." George replied.

Quickly, George reached into his back pocket, pulled out a grip of dog-eared papers, all printed out articles from the internet. Research he had done on his own. They were well worn, yellowed with age. George had been at this for a while.

"This is how I came to know about you. About Helen." He said.

With his wife's name mentioned, a chill ran through John. He didn't realize until that moment that he hadn't spoken her name aloud. In the four years past since she disappeared. When people would bring her up to express their condolences, it was always "your wife."

Helen's name on this man's tongue, a complete stranger who was beginning to sound a bit like a raving lunatic, caused him to pause. To choke back the sobs that threatened to break loose.

George spread the papers across the sticky, chipped table. Pointed to the top page.

It was a printout of a local newspaper. A headline in which he was all too familiar.

"Local Cop's Wife Missing."

George pointed to it. "This was my first introduction to your case. The first time I knew…"

He paused, unable to form the words.

John prodded.

"Knew? Knew what?"

George took a deep breath, tried to collect himself. "This was the first time I knew that it had happened again."

John's eyes narrowed, confused.

George spread the papers apart. To a more yellowed, weathered page. A printout from a headline further back.

1965.

"Elliott Marshall. 10 years old. Stumbled into town and claimed that his little brother, Sam, disappeared. They went fishing. Elliott started baiting his hook and by the time he turned around to his little brother to help him, he was gone. No footprints, nothing in the river. No screams, no cries, no blood. Nothing. Just… gone. He was never found."

John was intrigued now. He sat forward, looking down at the papers as George went through them, one by one.

He pointed to another article.

1953.

"Sarah Waters and Liam Noth. Went hiking with a large group of friends into the wilderness. According to their friends, Sarah and Liam were lagging behind, talking to each other, flirting. When they stopped to do a map check, Sarah and Liam were gone. Thinking they went off to find a secret place to neck, their friends called for them. Nothing. They finally went to the police station hours later, after searching on their own. The only thing they found was Liam's backpack. One ripped strap, no blood. They were never found."

John's brow furrowed as George went on. Another page, another. Another.

"1938. Lizzie MacGuire. Claims she's going to the nearby woods to collect wildflowers. She's never seen again. 1923. Jameson Smith. Kisses his wife on the forehead, tells her he's going to go hunting, never comes home. His gun was found 30 years later. Not a scratch or a spot of blood on it. It hadn't even been fired."

"Jesus," John whispered, staring at the huge stack of story after story of disappeared Rogue River citizens throughout the decades. George had been thorough. What drove him to begin this crusade, John didn't know. But he was more concerned with trying to wrap his mind around what George was telling him.

Finally, the question came. Soft and gentle, but urgent. Necessary. Important.

"John, do you have any reason to believe your wife wandered into the woods?"

John shook his head, unsure of much anymore. The firm relationship, the devout belief he'd had for all of those years that they had a great relationship, a solid marriage, dissipated when she disappeared. Day by day that she was gone, the doubt began to creep in.

His mind needed to make sense out of the unknowable. And he had to start coming to some hard truths, some hard honesties in his journey of figuring out what happened to her.

Perhaps she had more secrets than he had allowed himself to

believe.

"I don't know. I truly don't know," he answered George honestly. Truthfully. It was painful to say that he didn't know.

The woman he thought he knew everything about. Driving east towards Gold Hill the day she disappeared. Looking nervous, pre-occupied. Scared.

Had she later wandered into the woods? What led her out to Gold Hill?

For every clue he found, there seemed to be several more questions to answer.

A dark shadow passed over George's face. "These woods, this forest. It eats people. Swallows them whole. It's tainted land."

They both sat for a long moment, silent. The click of the pool table and the soft sounds of another classic rock ballad the only sounds in the bar. More people had milled into the bar during the 20 minutes they had been talking. No one paid them any mind.

John was the first to speak.

"What exactly do you mean by 'tainted land,' George?"

"For centuries, my people inhabited this area. I come from the Latgawa tribe, a little upland of here. My ancestors lived here for many years, until they were shuffled up north to a reservation. Stories were passed down from my parents, and my grandparents, and back and back. The war between our tribes and the local militia, even back then. My people didn't go anywhere near those woods."

"Why not? What was it that terrified you so much?"

George stared at John for a moment. He looked like he was silently deliberating with himself just how much he should tell. A moment later, he began shuffling through his papers again, his massive brown index finger pointing at an article that he had circled. And highlighted.

This page was more well-worn than most. Definitely one that he referenced often.

In the middle of the page, there was a small map of Rogue River and Gold Hill. A small piece of the map, north of Rogue River, was circled several times in bright red ink.

"Not all the woods, John," he pointed to the map. "Just these two miles."

John's eyes narrowed at the map. He'd circled a spot along Sardine Creek Road, remote and, as far as he knew, presently uninhabited.

"I know why you're here, John. In Gold Hill." George replied, catching his gaze, seriousness darkening his eyes. "I've seen you here before. I know why you come here, what you're searching for. You're looking for her."

John glanced downward, twirled his empty cup in his fingers, his lip trembling. He didn't want George to see how little he was managing to hold it all together. The truth was, he was always looking for her. In every crowd, his eyes would scour for her face. Every time the phone rang in the police station, he thought, for just a half second before he picked up the call, "This is it. They found her. Dumped somewhere. This is the end of a lifetime spent wondering, not knowing. It all ends now."

Inevitably, every call was about something else. Something unrelated. It kept him occupied. Busy. Graciously and mercifully so.

It took a random stranger, pointing these things out to him, saying his wife's name, reminding him that she was once very real, very warm, very human; not just the name, the obsession that he'd turned her into.

Any therapist in the world would tell him that his obsession with finding Helen tied directly into what happened with Jenny. Why he became a cop. Why he was dying inside a little bit every day. Every sunset, every sunrise, that passed by without fresh answers. No matter how sordid, how macabre, how vicious the answers may be, he longed for them.

Hungered for them.

Craved them.

He wanted to know. He needed to know. To move forward.

"I am," was all he managed to croak out.

"What is it about Gold Hill, John? Why do you come here? Did you see her come this direction the day she disappeared?" He asked, as gently as he could.

He nodded. "Yes, someone told me they saw her driving east that day. She could have gone farther, I suppose, than Gold Hill. She could have kept driving."

"But you don't believe that she did," George finished.

"To be honest, George. I'm not so sure I believe that anymore. But this is something. I guess, being here, it's something." John replied, realizing how damn pathetic he sounded, and hating it.

"Why don't we drive up there?" George asked, his mood shifted. He seemed eager, excited. But there was a dark edge to it. Almost as if it was something he knew must be done, yet he dreaded doing it. A destiny that had to be followed, no matter how dark the path may be.

John looked up at him, a stranger less than an hour ago, and now a trusted friend. He nodded, stood, threw a $20 bill on the table and

said, "Lead the way."

CHAPTER FOUR

OBSESSION

The trees drifted by quickly as they made their way north. George decided to drive as he knew the way. Early evening was upon them, and for a brief moment, John wondered if going out in the dark was the best course of action.

But he had to know. He had to see. He had to check. One glance over at George's profile, sturdy and strong and wise, and he knew that the obsession ran deep within his new friend as well. Something drove him to this patch of earth, the same way his obsession for answers was driven, he knew, by losing Jenny.

John rolled down the window, cranking the manual lever, to let in a little night air.

"Sorry it won't go lower," George replied. "My Bessie, she's a bit of an old girl," he said, patting the dashboard of the old car. It was an early model Hyundai. John wasn't even sure he'd seen that model before. It creaked and puffed smoke and made strange noises, but it seemed to be doing its job working and winding its way up the road. John let the cool Oregon evening breeze hit his face, closing his eyes briefly, relishing the fresh air. He heard some nocturnal birds beginning to sing their songs. Around him, the woods were alive, thriving with wildlife. Creatures.

Further they drove up Sardine Creek Drive, the road at one point turning into a dirt road, overgrown and unloved. Unremembered. Overhead, the canopy of the thick trees began to block out what little moonlight drifted down to them. It would have filled John with an even deeper sense of dread had it not been for the two utility flashlights he saw in the backseat of George's car.

"We may not find anything. In fact, it's more likely that we won't, John. But we have to try." George said after a long silence.

John nodded. "For what it's worth, thank you for coming out here with me."

George only shook his head slightly, his eyes still focused forward on the winding road before them. "I can't very well, in good conscience, let you come out here alone after I was the one who told you about it. If something were to happen to you… well, I don't want to live my life with any more regret." He replied softly, something lingering in the air between those words. Something damaged and painful.

John supposed George had his own stories, his own trials that he'd had to overcome. Or trials that he was still struggling to overcome.

Whatever led him to his obsession with these two miles, John was thankful for it. It was the first nibble, the first clue in a case that was already forgotten. Dismissed. Moved aside for more current business. And it may lead nowhere, John was aware of that fact. But, as George said, they had to try.

"We're getting close," George said, the map lying on the console next to him, his eyes drifting downward to reference.

"George, can I ask you something?" John began.

"Of course," he replied.

"This place, this two miles, with all of your research and years of figuring out precisely where it is, where it's concentrated... why haven't you come out here to investigate yourself?"

George was quiet as he shifted into a lower gear, the grade of the road elevating slightly. After a long moment, he replied, "This place, John... it terrifies me. I have my reasons. Let's just leave it at that, okay?"

John nodded solemnly, turning his gaze back to the window, the night growing deeper and darker around them.

"I wouldn't have the courage to come here alone. And you're the first person I've met that would have a reason to come out with me," he continued.

John turned to him. "Did you lose someone, George?"

George sighed, deep, pained. His voice cracked. "I've lost many someones, John. Many."

Before he had a chance to ask what that meant, George pulled the car to a sudden stop. They were stopped just on the gravel, over the crest of a hill, the brush almost intruding completely around the road. But it was the headlights, George's gaze focused straight ahead, and his sharp gasp that made John turn.

Stare.

What he saw caused a rivulet of fear to creep up his spine.

There, molded, dirty, covered by branches and underbrush that had encroached upon it slowly, sat Helen's Jeep.

August 1988

Port Townsend, Washington

Her room was kept sealed. Like a tomb. A tomb that her body

would never rest in.

John found his way in there one day, when he was sure his parents were downstairs. He shut the door quickly behind him, quietly. Looked around.

He was immediately assaulted with the pinks and the purples that hued her room. Pom poms from her drill team days hung from her mirror. Her mirror was littered with pictures, snapshots from fun days with Mary, lipstick kiss marks, and JSHAW written in makeup, a Blue Heron sticker next to it.

Her bed was still made, the paisley green and pink bedspread untouched. A thin layer of dust had begun to settle in the room, the air was stagnant. It hadn't seen sunlight or fresh air for a month. Diane came into the room in the mornings, made sure the windows were sealed, the curtains drawn. John thought it was her way of sealing the place, keeping it untouched from the outside world, waiting for the day Jenny would wander home, in her bright yellow sundress, her hair still swept up, her lips still glossy, and throw open the doors, like no time had passed. Like arriving now was the most natural thing in the world for her to do. No explanations, no scars, no pain, no death, no misery.

Just Jenny. In her bright yellow sundress.

February 2019

Two Miles

"Helen!" He screamed as he jumped out of the car, running up the pebble-filled road to her car. Or what was left of her car.

The windshield had been shattered irreparably, a huge branch resting in the middle of it. Moss and mold had grown all over the vehicle, encroaching undergrowth and brush had overcome the vehicle, reclaimed it back to nature, long ago. John knew it had been sitting there for years.

"Helen!! Baby!" John called, screaming, sobs breaking free from his lungs. That dim hope that he had so desperately clung to throughout the years, that she was alive, that she was safe somehow, sprang to life when he saw her Jeep. As beat up, as molded, as broken as it appeared to be, it was the first sign of her, of his Helen, that he'd had in years.

He flew over to the drivers' side door, which stood slightly open. Any battery that powered the Jeep had long ago died. He tried to peer inside but it was too dark.

"George! George, come quick!" He called, his tall friend lumbering awkwardly, bringing with him the two flashlights. He turned one on and handed it to John.

John threw the cone of light over the insides of the Jeep. An old plastic water bottle in the console, half gone. Spider webs laced the interior windows, making their new home in the relative comforts of the Jeep.

His eyes fell to the floor of the passenger side of the Jeep. His skin crawled and he uttered a despaired, "Fuck."

"What is it?" George asked, nervously standing next to John near the open door of the Jeep. He kept turning his face back to the maw of the forest surrounding them. As if watching for somebody. Waiting for someone.

"Her purse is here," John replied, his stomach sinking.

He knew, deep down, that if she was alive, she would have taken her purse with her. Its presence in her Jeep sent him into yet another downward tailspin. Somehow the despair was even darker the second time; having that brief run from the car to the Jeep, seeing his first clue, his first piece of evidence of Helen after four long years, had given him a brief glimmer of hope. And it was even darker, even more rank, when it was ripped from him the second time.

He grabbed the purse, a spider scrambling out nervously from underneath it and disappeared.

John blew a thin layer of dust off of it, opened it up. Her wallet and cell phone were still in the purse. Her keys were nowhere to be found.

John crawled out, flashed the light around the edges of the forest, thick and uninviting. Sable black.

"Helen! Are you there?!" He called, his voice cracking. George shone his light into the edge of the woods as well, searching for any sign of anything unusual.

The woods were quiet. Unnaturally quiet. He couldn't even hear the birds. It felt like this tiny little part of the world was a cave, pushing out the sounds of anything beyond it. Claustrophobically small. Binding. Trapping.

John started to run into the woods but George caught his arm immediately. He gave a grave look to John and said, "I don't think that would be wise, John."

John ripped his arm away. Glared at George in anger.

"This is the first clue I've found in four goddamn years. Of course,

I have to search! Of course, I have to look! I need to know, George, I need to know!"

"And you will. You will. But I don't think ripping into the woods with just a flashlight and no idea where to begin looking is the best idea. Chances are good that… I mean… It has been four years, John."

It took all of John's best efforts to swallow down the lump that was rising in his throat, to keep his feet precisely where they stood instead of running off into the darkness, calling her name, leaving George far behind. But he knew what George was saying made sense.

He stood in the woods for a moment more, waiting for a reply. A call in the night. A reply from his wife. Even though in his head, her even being alive made no logical sense, this was still what he stood waiting for in the cold Oregon evening.

Waiting. Even now. Still waiting.

Waiting for her to come home. Waiting to hear what happened. Waiting to know. Waiting again.

Waiting.

Waiting.

Waiting.

John groaned and replied, "You're right. I know you're right,

George. But she's out there. I've waited so long. I've come so far.
What's a little walk through the woods going to hurt?"

"That's what it wants you to think."

For the first time since he got out of the car, John turned to him,
his eyebrows furrowed in confusion.

"*It?*"

George averted his eyes, didn't meet his gaze. Changed the subject
entirely.

"We'll go back home tonight. We'll rest up. Come out here first
thing in the morning. Take advantage of the light. Come prepared.
Set our bearings. Our boundaries. Draw up a game plan. A strategy.
And if she's out there, John. She will be found. This I promise you."

Despite a wealth of questions, especially the big one that hung
unanswered in the air, John nodded silently.

Walked back to the car. Complied and crawled back in.

As the headlights washed over the Jeep again, forgotten and
neglected under the invading nature of the area, John knew.

That no matter what happened tomorrow, whether the danger, the
mysterious "it" that George so aptly let slip, would kill him… no
matter what happened, he would find what he was looking for.

He would find what he was looking for.

TWO MILES

CHAPTER FIVE

SUPERSTITIONS

Tall Trees sat in his living room, darkened and sparsely decorated. A single light from the kitchen sent a small cone of illumination into the cramped apartment.

The night had been long, disappointing. But it bore some fruit. John was reassured of where Helen had gone the night she disappeared.

Tall Trees was not reassured at all.

He turned on the television. The only thing on that late at night was a foreign soccer game. He twirled a rabbit's foot around and around his fingertips, staring at it thoughtfully, the game already forgotten.

How long had been doing this? How long had the search lasted?

He got up and moved over to the small deck of cards that he kept on a nearby bookcase. Caressed them for a moment, appreciating the solid quality of the cards. Leather bound. Expensive.

Old.

He sat back down on his cramped sofa, his long legs sticking out and awkwardly bumping the coffee table. Tall Trees put down the rabbit's foot and shuffled the deck.

He knew he would not survive this. That he most likely would not survive what was to come. Of that he was sure.

But he wanted to hear it. Regardless. To know that he was on the right path.

He shut his eyes, cleared his throat, took a deep breath. Asked aloud, to the room and anyone who was listening, "What will tomorrow bring?"

His fingers worked to the depths of the deck, drawing a single card.

With a moment of reflection, he finally turned the card over.

And his stomach fell with what he saw there.

An owl.

He dreamed.

He slept deeply and dreamed vividly.

It was a memory, a remnant of a lifetime before. All that he took with him in those days were the memories and the pain.

He was much younger; waking up in his tent to the sounds of laughter, light conversation. He unzipped the tent and saw his father, mother and brother awake, sitting around a fire, drinking coffee.

His father turned in his direction; saw that he was awake.

"Good morning, son." Eagle Calls greeted him.

He smiled in reply. Stumbled out and joined his family around the campfire.

Tall Trees had grown up on a reservation near Salem, Grand Ronde. Most of the Takelma and Latgawa tribes were relocated to the reservation and that was the only life Tall Trees knew. His father was Latgawa and his mother was white. To better acclimate himself to his European heritage, he received a Christian name in addition to the Latgawan name.

His father, Eagle Calls, went by Simon.

But this was a special trip.

A very special trip.

His father was dying.

"Darling, did you want some coffee?" His mother asked, and he nodded.

His parents met and fell in love during a time when it was frowned upon to do so. Her parents were so disapproving that she left, and they made the long journey back south down to the place of his people, his tribe. A few had managed to trickle back down to Rogue River from the reservation up north. But others scattered to the winds.

Simon had received word the previous week that his cancer was back. With a vengeance. Knowledge was limited in regards to treatment, so Simon knew he was living on borrowed time.

He wanted to take his boys to the woods, on a hunting expedition.

Simon kept it from the boys: he didn't want to cause any worry.

But George knew. He'd heard his parents talking one night. And it sounded grim.

Heritage and culture was big for Simon. The dilution of his people from the lands his ancestors groomed and called home made it even harder. He wanted his boys to know as much about the Latgawa as possible. He knew once he was gone, they would be reared American. It was now or never.

"Grab your bows. Your mother will stay to watch the camp. Let's see if we can catch some of the deer drinking down near the creek." Eagle Calls said, grabbing his own bow and quiver.

George did as he was bid. As excited as he was to be out in the wild with his father, as eager as he was to learn the ways of his people, he couldn't shake the terrible dread that permeated his heart.

This was the first and the last time.

The first and the last.

He threw a wave to his mother over his shoulder. She smiled at him and started cleaning up the coffee cups. Into the woods they went.

The creek was about a half a mile from their campsite. As they neared closer, they all crouched and slowly crept up to the water's edge, as Simon instructed.

They sat in the brush for a while, waiting for animals to come and drink. But nothing came.

Simon sighed out of frustration. "Where are the deer? They have to drink," he said.

George turned to his father.

"Maybe if I go a little further upstream. About 50 yards. Worth a check."

Simon smiled at him. Ran a hand through his thick black hair.

"Like I showed you, then," he replied. "Keep low, keep soft-footed, keep quiet."

George nodded and began to move. Though he was a tall, weighty adolescent, somehow he was able to move through the forest lithe, quickly, silently. The brush hardly shook when he moved into position about 50 yards away from where his brother and father sat.

He turned to wave them over.

But they were gone.

George stood up slightly, trying to get a better viewpoint of the tops of the bushes. He waved his hand in the air, no longer concerned about startling the non-existent wildlife.

Nothing.

Concerned, he stood and made his way back over to the bushes.

Gone.

They were gone.

"Dad? Eddie?" He called out to his father and brother. Maybe he misjudged how far upstream he had gone. Maybe he had the wrong bush.

He began to run further downstream when something caught his eye.

His brother's bow. Broken in half. Lying in the bushes.

"Dad! Eddie!" He called, the silence of the forest seeming to throw his voice back in his face. Everything was diluted here. Deafeningly silent.

"Where are you?" He called, worried. He began to run back in the direction of the camp. Maybe they were there. If not, they would definitely know to meet him there should they get separated.

"Mom! Are Dad and Eddie with you?" He called as he approached the camp. He could see the tent from a distance, he was getting closer. His long legs were pumping so hard he thought his lungs would explode.

As he rounded the corner into the campsite, he couldn't find his Mom.

"Mom? Are you here?" He called, looking around worriedly. George rounded a corner and saw a red blanket on the ground.

He stopped.

Stared.

His blood ran cold.

It wasn't a blanket.

It was his mother's body.

Her neck was ripped clean off her neck.

His knees felt wobbly and he collapsed in sobs. His gaze was pulled to something higher, higher...

Up in a tree, about 9 feet above him, was her head.

A stick plunged deep into the base of her skull.

CHAPTER SIX

CLANDESTINE

It was almost one in the morning when he finally stumbled into the dark house. He threw his keys and the purse on the console table and knelt on the top of it, steadying himself. His gaze drifted up to the mirror, studying his reflection.

John had dark circles under his eyes, wrinkles beginning to crease his skin. Gray began to freckle his hair. The last four years had not been kind to him.

Eleanor had been the worst. Eventually, after the first year of Helen missing, they arranged to have a memorial service. Or what Eleanor called, "A Celebration of Life." John was against it. He couldn't bring himself to admit that she was gone. Eleanor fought him on it every step of the way and she won.

The reception was held at his house. Mourners dressed in black milled around, no more the ghosts or the ghastly faces of disbelief. Those days were long passed. Instead they were more accusatory stares in his direction. Inquisitive gazes, trying to bore holes into him, break free the well of secrets that he must surely be keeping. No grown woman, especially Helen Shaw, would get up and walk out. There had to be foul play involved, most of them, he was certain, had determined in their minds. He had to be guilty.

If not in the act of murdering her himself, the act of driving her away. The act of being an absentee, horrible husband.

The dead are often held on pedestals that will never be knocked down. He knew that now.

He went around to the group anyway, a mix of family and friends, relatives both distant and near, that he hadn't seen in a long while. Thanked them for coming. Turned around and heard the whispers, the hushed conversations, creating drama where virtually none existed. At least, none that he was aware of. Again, his mysterious Helen. Questions abound.

"He has to know something. He has to know what happened to her."

"I bet he did it himself. Or hired someone to do it."

"I didn't think he would injure a flea. But now I'm not so sure. How could she just disappear without a trace? Helen would never do that."

Eleanor was in the center of it, dressed in a sharp black pantsuit, her hair drawn up in a severe bun. She had a gathering, a gaggle of well wishers around her constantly, while he had to actively get up and circulate to speak to anyone.

At one point he shut himself away on the sunporch. Reached into his pocket to pull out his stash of emergency cigarettes. He didn't generally smoke, but today…

The door opened to the sunporch and his parents filed out. Diane gave him a wan smile and sat down in a folding chair next to him. Put a hand on his knee. His father leaned against the wall, crossing his arms, obviously uncomfortable in the grey suit he had been forced to wear.

"Hi Johnny, baby. How you holding up?" She asked, concern creasing her eyes.

He took a long draw from his cigarette, turned his head to avoid blowing smoke near his Mom. "Honestly? I have no idea. It's been a year, Mom. And I still have no idea."

Diane simply nodded, looking down to her lap and then over to Alan, who avoided her gaze. Now that John was old enough to see things clearly, he could tell that the loss of Jenny was hard on his parent's relationship. They were there for each other, continued to be there for each other, but there were the unspoken things. The things they never dared utter aloud to each other, let alone let fly in front of him. The unanswered questions about that specific day. That July.

There was blame there. Unannounced blame. It seeped along the edges like a cancer. John could see it. Black and cankerous and festering. They blamed each other. Diane and Alan couldn't face it, couldn't handle what speaking it aloud would do to them. So, it sat. Undealt with. Unhandled.

Unresolved.

And they never moved on.

Jenny's bedroom was still very much sealed up, dustier, frillier than he remembered. Sealed up for a woman of almost 40 years old to come home to. The drill team pom poms, the mascot stickers, the bright 80s makeup.

The obsession was inherited, John realized. The obsession was contagious.

"I'm forgetting what she sounded like," John spoke, taking another draw from the cigarette.

Diane smiled. Put her hands in her lap primly. "Not me. That's one thing I can remember, that I can take with me. Jenny's laugh. Infectious." She smiled broadly at the thought, her eyes thick with memories.

John turned to her, studied her for a moment. Gently replied, "I was talking about Helen, Mom."

Broken from her reverie, Diane's eyes brimmed with tears. She managed a wan smile, shaky, and giggled lightly. "Oh. I apologize."

And suddenly John's heart hurt so deeply for his parents. What he lost, he would never be able to move past, not until he got the answers that he needed. But his parents. They had suffered much more. A child they brought into the world, spent their lives trying to rear and grow and protect, being ripped from them by someone or something unknown, something unknowable...

His heart hurt very deeply for his parents in that moment. He looked over to Alan who was glancing down, avoiding his gaze. He looked annoyed, frustrated by Diane's gaff. John put his hand over his mother's. Gave her a smile.

Eleanor came out onto the porch then. Her usual cold cordiality particularly icy.

"Alan, Diane, would you mind if I stole your son for a moment?" She asked in her haughty, pretentious air.

The sad choice of words threw Diane off yet again, and she gasped and then giggled in spite of herself. To Eleanor, John imagined she looked mad.

"Of course, dear. He's all yours." Diane replied, those tears threatening to break loose over her eyes steadfastly strong. Unrelenting.

For all of his mother's weaknesses, John admired this about her. She would never give Eleanor the satisfaction of seeing her cry.

John ground out the cigarette on the bottom of his heel. He kissed his Mom on the forehead and squeezed his Dad's shoulder lightly as he walked into the kitchen with Eleanor.

She pulled him aside immediately and said, "Is everything alright with your mother? We can't have emotional theatrics today. Please make sure she stays out on the sundeck if she has to cry."

"Eleanor…" John began, the anger rising in him.

But before he could reply, she had walked away, back into the throng of mourners and well-wishers.

He went to his bedroom, dark and cool with the shades drawn, and shut the door behind him. Flung himself on his bed and grabbed the framed wedding photo on his nightstand.

She wore a simple lace dress that day. Her blonde hair was bound up loosely in a chignon. It became loose throughout the day and she undid it before the reception and shook her long hair loose. That was what he loved about her most.

She wasn't the type of woman to thrive in the details. In perfection. Helen was unlike her mother in that way. Eleanor was resolute in everything. Planned, thorough, focusing on the minutiae of everything. Helen was more of a free spirit. She wanted to live life. She didn't have to be perfect.

Even early on in their relationship, when he told her about Jenny, she sat cross-legged in front of him, a glass of red wine near her lips, one hand on his knee. She gave him his time. She let him work up to it. And after he told her everything, she held him. Kissed his neck. Whispered in his ear.

"I'm so sorry, John. She sounded like a wonderful sister. But know this: however lost you've been feeling since then, however ungrounded, however desperate you are for answers… you have a home now. I am your home, baby. And I'm not going anywhere."

He smiled weakly, grabbed the sides of her face, his thumb lightly tracing her lips, still moist with red wine, and kissed her. She always knew just what to say to him. Every glance, every word, every breath filled him with life whenever she was near.

"I'm not going anywhere..." Her words echoed through the cavernous empty house and he slammed his fist through the mirror. Glass shattered and blood began to drip down to the floor. He didn't care.

He stared up at his reflection, muddled and unrecognizable and began to cry.

"Why did you leave me? Why, Helen?" His sobs ripped through his throat, already raw from having cried so many tears for her over the years. John was exhausted. Torn. Ready to move forward with some semblance of a life.

But he needed to know. His obsession drove him forward illogically. It made no sense. He just had to know. He had to understand.

"Why were you out in the woods, baby? Why? What happened?"

It felt like, at every turn, for every answer he got, ten more questions lined up behind it. He knew that Helen took off that day, likely with every intention of going exactly where she did. The casserole was still in the oven. She wasn't expecting to be gone long.

This is good, this is good, he told himself silently, his mind slowly going through the facts logically, processing them. He began to pace around the foyer of the house, his fist dripping blood rivulets to the gray carpet below. He hardly noticed.

She gets in the Jeep, he thought to himself. She begins to make her way to the store. But she doesn't make it. We know that much because Mitzy, the cashier, never saw her. The only person that saw her was the gas station clerk. Pumping up gas, looking worried, concerned, frightened, but alone. Around 5:30pm.

And we know where she went. She drove up to Two Miles, parked, left her purse and cell phone...

Cell phone.

Like a shot he grabbed the purse from the console table and went to the bedroom. Helen had an outdated cell phone that he wasn't sure he had a cord for anymore. He'd need to charge it to turn it on.

He went into the office and dove into the junk drawer, his

fingers parsing through lots of unknown AC adapters and other cords. Realizing he was dripping blood everywhere, he muttered, a "Shit," and went to the bathroom to bandage it. Luckily, it wasn't very deep. A little alcohol and a bandage and he was back in the office, going through drawer after drawer of cords.

Power cords for laptops he no longer had, an old camcorder that he hardly ever used.

Finally, he found one that looked like it might fit. He plugged it into the wall and waited for a moment, the screen on the phone still completely black.

After a moment, a little "low power" icon clicked on and he sighed, relieved. He'd have to give it a while to juice up.

Exhausted, he collapsed on the bed, not sure he'd be able to get any shut eye.

He was asleep as soon as his head hit the pillow.

John's eyes opened, the gray early morning dawn beginning to peek through the curtains, and he sat up quickly.

The phone.

He scrambled up and picked up the phone. Fully charged.

Luckily she didn't keep a passcode on the phone. The first thing he swiped into was her text messages.

The usual rundown of messages between her and John. Asking what time he'd be home, if he could remember to pick up his dry cleaning, letting him know she DVR'd his favorite shows. Nothing riveting.

The last text she sent to him was the morning she disappeared, after he had already arrived at work. He never kept his cell on him during his shift and she knew that. It was just a two-word text. Simple.

Haunting.

"Love you."

A random message sent to him the morning that she disappeared. John might be biased, but he had been an officer for many years and he didn't think that sounded like a woman who was determined to leave her husband.

Then he moved to the Call Log. All incoming and outgoing calls made on the phone.

Most of them were familiar. Eleanor. Daniel's cell. Home. John's cell. A girlfriend she'd made at a cooking class she took a few years ago.

But then he noticed the call he was looking for, marked Unknown.

It called her at 5:24pm. The call lasted about a minute.

John stood staring at that word, "Unknown" for the longest time, as if his eyes boring into that word could somehow draw up a number, a lead, something for him to follow up on.

Unknown. Could this be it? The difference between her driving to the store and making a trip to Gold Hill? Who was this?

His mind flashed to an affair. Perhaps she was seeing another guy. Maybe she wasn't as happy with the marriage as he thought. Maybe Helen had her secrets.

But deep down, in some part of himself that he couldn't identify, he knew that wasn't true. It wasn't that he was a perfect husband. Or that Helen was a perfect wife. Either one of them could slip. Take a bad moment in time in their relationship, make a mistake.

But something told John there was more here.

Something more.

He flipped through her photos. Standard pictures of him, of her, candid shots of the both of them together, photos of her rose garden, the dishes she'd prepared for dinner after taking her cooking class.

Nothing clandestine.

Nothing illicit.

John looked up at the clock. He knew he needed to leave to meet with George. He began to close down the open apps and noticed one that was still open.

One that he hadn't opened. One that Helen must have. That day.

Curious, he opened it up and realized it was an audio recording app.

His heart beating fast, beads of sweat beginning to run down his face, he pressed Play.

TWO MILES

CHAPTER SEVEN

THE ONES THAT CAME BEFORE

July 1988

Port Townsend, Washington

"Wake up, doofus," he heard her say.

His eyes opened, little traitors that they were, and he pushed her. "Get off me, you dork."

She giggled. "Come on, Bub. Mom said to get up." Jenny rose to go.

He called her back.

"Jenny?"

She turned. "Yeah?"

She was walking through the door. Halfway through the door. Soon barbecues would be in full swing, lawn mowers would be whirring, children running around, fireworks being prepped.

And she would be gone.

And the rest of his life would be a nightmare because of it.

"Jenny. Jenny, don't go."

She contorted her face and smiled. "Okay, Bub, you're being uncharacteristically needy today. We're supposed to hate each other, remember? Mortal enemies and all that?" She laughed, but she took a few more steps into the room. Closer to him.

"I just... I have a feeling."

Her smile froze for a moment, suspended in confusion. She studied silently for a long while. Then she chuckled. "Well, I'm stoked for you and your feelings, Bub. Proves you're not an emotionless robot. Which means my entire theory about you is wrong."

She joked again, moving closer to the door.

"Something bad is going to happen!" He called out, desperately. Somehow, somehow, he was back in his childhood bedroom, on that fateful morning, with all he knew now... pleading for her to stay. Pleading for her to remain.

She should have had a life. A husband. A gaggle of babies. A career. College. A future.

And he should have had a sister.

She stopped. Stared at him, concerned. No longer merriment around the edges.

She moved over to the bed and sat down.

"Bub, nothing's going to happen to me, okay? I'm going to be fine. I promise."

"No, you're not." He replied, matter-of-factly.

Her gaze narrowed again. "How could you possibly know that for sure?"

It was a question he couldn't answer. All he could think, as he lay in his childhood bed, in his childhood room, and his voice squeaked out with the adolescent timbre of his youth, maybe this was a second chance? A chance to stop it before it starts.

"I just do," was all that he could manage. It was all he could say.

Her smile quivered its way back across her lips. She leaned down closer to him.

"How about this, Bub? How about I promise you that I'll be careful? That I won't let anything happen to me, okay?"

Knowing she couldn't make a promise like that, couldn't possibly keep a promise like that, but maybe she didn't have to. Maybe, he thought, she'd be extra vigilant tonight. Maybe she would be more careful because of what he said.

He nodded a silent reply.

She smiled and kissed him on the forehead. "I do love you, you pain in the ass. You know that, right?"

Again, a silent nod. Tears welling up. He knew she would be gone before they would begin to fall.

She squeezed his hand lightly, got up and was gone.

Out the door.

And into the deceptively harmless day.

February 2019

Rogue River, Oregon

They agreed to meet up at The Elks Café in Gold Hill that morning for breakfast. John was already on his second cup of coffee when George walked through the door. He slid across John in the booth and motioned to the waitress for a cup of coffee.

"Good morning," John began. He wore a baseball hat over his face. His eyes were bloodshot. He didn't want George to know how bad a night and morning he'd had thus far.

George looked pretty much the same, John thought to himself. His friend had bags under his brown eyes, his face looked haggard and drawn. Neither one of them appeared to have had a good night.

John waited for the waitress to serve the coffee and take their orders for breakfast before he started.

Before he could start, George cut him off. "I have something I need to share with you."

John, a little puzzled, just nodded and waited for him to continue.

"I… When I was…" He sighed, struggling to find the words.

"It's okay, man. You can tell me." John said.

George took a deep breath. "There's something in those woods, John."

"What do you mean, 'something?'" He asked.

"Something foul. Something ancient and diabolical. Something strong and massive and just fucking hungry."

"What… what are you talking about?" John asked, confused.

"I haven't told you everything. About why I need to go back there. About what's driving me back there. And it's not easy to do. It's not easy to talk about."

John was about to say something, but the plates of food came. Neither of them seemed interested in the steaming food in front of them.

"It's okay. You can tell me," John prodded.

"My mother was murdered in those woods."

John's eyes widened.

"My mother was murdered by something. I don't know what. Stealthy and massive and strong. I never heard her cry out. It… John, it ripped her head clean off. Nailed it to a tree trunk nine feet high."

John's skin grew cold. He shivered despite the crowded restaurant being more than warm enough. Why hadn't he thought of it before? Beth Murdoch. Her story about her ancestor Henry was eerily similar.

Suddenly he had an idea.

"George, do you have a sleeping bag?"

He seemed a little surprised that the subject changed so quickly after such a weighty admission. George choked out a, "Yes, at my apartment."

"Let's grab enough gear for a couple of nights. And we have

one last stop before we head up to Two Miles."

George was stunned, but just nodded. They threw some money down on the table and left.

Twenty minutes later, they pulled up to Elizabeth's small duplex. Across the street, Dirk was standing out in his yard, leaning on his aluminum fence, keeping an ever vigilant eye out for Dexter.

John waved a greeting in his direction and ignored the beginning of Dirk's diatribe. He didn't have time to listen to that now. George emerged from the vehicle and Dirk quickly shut up. He eyed the massive Native American man, and quickly turned around and went into his house.

John noticed. Laughed.

"I ought to bring you around with me more often, George."

George laughed.

John rapped quickly on Elizabeth's door. It opened and she saw John's face.

"Look it, now, that asshole has nothing to complain about. I've started taking Dex to the bathroom in the backyard, so I don't know what…"

She trailed off when her eyes moved over to the tall man standing next to him.

"Well, hello," she replied, a tone in her greeting that sounded a little bit friendlier than she usually greeted her guests.

George ignored it and nodded.

"Can we come in?" John asked.

"Absolutely." She replied, her eyes still very much on George. She moved aside but took him in with her gaze. John could tell George was a little embarrassed by the rapt attention.

They both sat down on the sofa across from her, George's knees bumping the coffee table in front of him. Elizabeth noticed and smiled.

John began. "I didn't come here about Dirk. I actually came here about the conversation we had a long time ago. Do you remember? About Henry?"

Immediately her eyes shot up to the picture, that was dusty and still sitting up on the mantlepiece where it had always been. "Yes, of course. What about him?"

John shot a glance to George.

"Do you remember what you told me? About how they found the dogs? Pinned to the tree?" He started, cautious around the sensitivity of the conversation. He could feel George tense up on the sofa.

"Yes, their heads were pinned to the tree trunks."

George shot a gaze over to John, and then back to Elizabeth. "What is this now?" He asked.

Elizabeth began to retell the story, although she had more passion and fire in her eyes telling the story this time to George than she did originally a few years back.

When she was done, John asked, "Elizabeth, this is very important. Do you happen to know where his cabin was?"

She looked confused but didn't ask any additional probing questions. "Sure, I think I might. If I had a map…"

Out of his pocket, quicker than a flash, George produced his old tattered rag of a map and laid it down on the coffee table.

Elizabeth grinned. She began to point to the map.

"This area right here, that's where the cabin is," she replied.

John and George both looked at each other in horror and shock.

Though neither of them was particularly shocked.

The cabin was within Two Miles.

After leaving a very confused Elizabeth, both George and John sat in his cruiser. George was the first to break the silence.

"I didn't get to finish my story in the café, John. My father and brother were in the woods with me that day too. But they vanished. I was scoping out a spot for a hunt along the creek bed but when I turned back, they were gone. I believe my Mom…" He choked back a sob.

"I believe my Mom was left as a warning."

"A warning? By what?" John asked, knowing that he both wanted to know the answer and didn't want to know the answer. Both in equal measure.

"My people called them, 'The Ones that Came Before.'"

John listened, silently.

"They believed in beasts that haunted the woods near Two Miles, that gave off a scent so foul and minute that only other animals could smell. It deterred them from entering their realm. Kept other animals away. And it grew hungry. Though it hibernated. Only needed to feed every few years or so. Some of my people believe it had a supernatural origin. Or supernatural powers. I think it's as simple a mystery as a hungry beast that has been killing for centuries."

John sat silently for the longest time. Trying to process everything that he was hearing. Everything that was being said.

"So, you think there is a simple explanation for this?" John asked.

"Yes."

"You think a Sasquatch or some horribly deformed hybrid monster is stalking the woods and eating people?"

Meekly, he replied, "Yes."

"You don't think there's anything going on in those woods that isn't readily explainable?"

"No, I think it's all easily explained."

He sighed deeply. Lowered his head.

"George, I think I should let you hear something."

George's heart sank a little bit. "What is it?"

John reached into his back pocket and pulled out a phone. "This was Helen's. It was in her purse when we found the Jeep. I went through it and found some interesting things."

"Like what?" George asked, his interest piqued.

"She got a call the night she disappeared. From an unknown number. At first, I thought it might have been another guy. That she might have taken off and run away with some other fella. But then I saw something else."

He handed the phone over to George. "What is it?" He asked again, feeling like a broken record.

"She must have recorded it halfway into the call. I only have about 10 seconds when the call lasted for a full minute. Hit Play."

Obediently, George turned back to the phone in his hand and hit the Play button.

"....tell him... tell him where to find me. Tell him to come and get me. Tell Bub I love him and I need him... I need help, Helen. Help!"

The voice was muddled, strangely garbled. The quality of the recording wasn't top quality. But it was the voice he heard. The message. That made his blood run cold.

"I don't understand, John. Who is that?" George asked.

"That is my sister, Jenny. She's been missing for 22 years."

TWO MILES

CHAPTER EIGHT

TALL TREES

His desire for truth was what led him out here. He was about to sacrifice everything to find out what happened to his wife. Ready to sacrifice everything. He simply had to know.

He had pieced it together in his mind that morning before George arrived at the café.

Helen left a note, a casserole baking and went to the store for milk. She got a call from a number she didn't recognize.

She knew who Jenny was. John had told her many times. Usually after beer-filled evenings, alcohol tainted confessions, when the emotions seemed much further away, much further out of grasp, a bit less difficult to verbalize. But they were always raw, and his wife understood how deeply he loved his sister.

Whoever it was that called Helen, John wasn't completely sold that it was truly his sister, lured her to the forest. He never carried his cell phone on the job and the station house would just go to voicemail when they were on their rounds. Helen knew this. By the time she probably had her mind in the right place to send a text message, after gassing up at the station on her way to Gold Hill, she wasn't able to get service. Gold Hill was notoriously bad for cell reception.

Helen Shaw.

Her heart as pure as gold.

Got a call for help and she rushed out into the fray.

Every bad thing that was uttered about him, every rumor, every whisper that he murdered her, his beloved wife, all came crashing around his shoulders. His own guilt of even doubting her, for the split second of moments, doubting her devotion to him, her loyalty to him, was something he knew he would have to live with for the rest of his life.

However long that was going to last, anyway.

The drive up to Two Miles was subdued, quiet. Both had a lot to digest.

George had grabbed a shotgun along with his sleeping bag. John still had his Glock 22 by his side, though he knew if the thing was as huge as George suspected, it wouldn't do much more than stun it. Still, it was something.

The plan was to find the cabin, spend the night, wait for it to come.

Whatever *it* was.

"Here we go," George said as he pulled off to the side of the road. He grabbed his grubby map and checked to be sure.

"Lord, I've got to get you a GPS or something, George," John said, smiling at his friend. "Lucky for us both, I've got my compass." He said as he produced it from his pocket.

It was George's turn to laugh. "Did you get that in the Boy Scouts?"

John laughed, turned it over in his head, cheap and plastic but durable. "Yeah, maybe." He glanced around. "Where are we anyway?"

"According to my map, the cabin should be about a half mile in from here. You ready?"

"As ready as I'm going to be," John replied, and opened the door. A few minutes later, they were walking into the woods, their backpacks and sleeping bags in tow. Dusk was just starting to fall. The day had gotten away from them with all of the unexpected stops they made. John had hoped to get to the cabin before nightfall and they were still on track.

"Do you hear that?" George asked after a few minutes.

John stopped, listened.

"No, I don't hear anything." He replied.

"Exactly." George said. He looked down to his arms, the black hair beginning to rise. John felt a strange static electricity in the air as well. Something almost imperceptible. It got stronger the further they walked into the woods.

It felt almost hard to breathe. He remembered grabbing a wool blanket when he was younger. He was playing hide and seek with Jenny. He'd throw the blanket over his head and immediately felt warm. Surrounded. Itchy. Heavy.

The air was alive here. It felt a lot like that wool blanket.

Suffocating.

They rounded a corner and found a small log cabin standing a few hundred yards away. Massive trees stood as pillars against the outside. The cabin was covered with moss and greenery. Had they not been looking for it, John doubted they would have seen it.

"Is this it?" John asked, turning to George who was busy studying his map.

"Yeah, this looks to be it."

John glanced at the small log cabin, saw the barrel sitting out front, the table beside it. Yes, this was the cabin from the photograph. He was sure of it.

He opened the door and immediately coughed by the uprising of dust that came in his wake. The cabin was no larger than a small bedroom. A small woodstove on one end, a small bed against the corner, and a table for preparing and curing furs. There were a few logs left next to the stove and John immediately went to work building a fire.

George set his pack down, leaned the shotgun against the wall, and glanced around.

"You can have the bed, George," John volunteered. "I can park it on the floor."

George laughed. "You kidding? That thing looks like it was built for an... um.... slightly shorter guy. My legs would hang over the side of that thing and I'd likely kick the lantern over and start a fire."

John laughed and glanced up at George. "You really are a doomsday kind of guy, aren't you?"

George just smiled quietly and began to unroll his sleeping bag.

After they started a fire, keeping it going through the night a log at a time, both of them curled up for what would likely be an uncomfortable evening of rest.

In the dark, George spoke.

"You know, my people, they believed that these creatures, the Ones that Came Before… that they had supernatural powers."

John nodded in the dark, that went unnoticed. He spoke.

"You mentioned that, yeah. What kind of powers did they supposedly have?"

George took a moment and then continued. "Some people believed they had the ability to become invisible. And others believed that they were part of another realm. Another plane of existence entirely. Maybe… Maybe, it's a little bit of both, John."

"What do you mean?" John asked, his voice hovering in the dark.

"What if this thing… steals people. Steals them. Maybe this is why there are no bones, no remains, nothing has been recovered of those that have gone missing. Maybe these people aren't dead. Just… in another realm."

John didn't respond. He just lay there quietly, considering.

A week ago, if Tall Trees had come to him, spouting off this exact type of garbage, he would have locked him up for the night, convinced he was either insane or drunk. Or both. But after everything he'd seen since then, he was opening his mind to other possibilities. Because the ones that were written in the scientific books just didn't seem to apply here.

"Last night I drew an Owl card." George said.

"George, buddy, I'm having a hard time keeping up with you, here. What do you mean, 'you drew an Owl card?'"

"I asked what was in store for tomorrow, and I drew an Owl card. In my culture, the owl symbolizes death."

"That's cheerful," John replied. "Have you ever found your cards to be wrong?"

"No. They never have been. So, I'm lying here, drifting off to sleep on what could be my last night on earth. I just want you to know, John. My goal is to help you find out what happened to your wife. I've given up on ever finding any answers on my family long ago."

John shifted in the dark, turned towards him and propped his head up in his hand. "You mean, you only came out here to help me find my wife? You're only out here for me?"

Softly, from the darkness, he replied, "Yes. I've seen this thing tear families apart for years. I want it stopped."

John fell back against the dusty pillow, his eyes welling with tears yet again.

"For what it's worth, George. I really do hope you find what you're looking for." John said.

He was quiet a moment before he replied.

"That's just the thing, John. I hope I don't."

CHAPTER NINE

UNKNOWABLE

John woke up with a start. In the darkness, George breathed deeply, heavily, steadily. He lay in the dark for a moment, wondering what caused him to awaken. And then he heard it again.

And his blood chilled.

A child's laughter. A little boy. Out in the dark. In the thick of these dizzying woods.

"George, did you hear that?" He called out to his friend. George didn't stir.

"George! George, wake up!" He called louder, standing up and slipping his on his jacket.

The laughter came again, this time much closer to the cabin. John grabbed a flashlight and his Glock.

"George! Get up!" He moved over to his friend, whose chest raised up and down steadily in the darkness. But he didn't stir. It was unnaturally sedate. John was terrified.

The laughter again. John knew that if there was truly a child in the woods, he'd need to help him immediately. Lead him back to wherever he came from.

Cautiously, John opened the cabin door, shining his flashlight into the darkness.

"Hello?" He called out to the dark. "Little boy?"

Slowly he stepped away from the fading heat of the cabin, into the cold air of the Oregon night. He shut the door behind him, his hand moving instinctively to the Glock at his side.

His fast awakening mind knew something wasn't right. Logically, it didn't make sense to wake up deep in the woods and hear a child's laughter. If this child was truly lost, John very much doubted that he would be laughing.

John heard a rustle of brush off to his right. He turned, aimed the flashlight to the bush.

Nothing.

"Hello? Are you there, little guy?" He called again, his breath coming out in front of him in plumes.

He moved deeper into the woods, trying to listen to the deafening darkness, waiting for the sound of the child to come again. Eventually it did, off to his left, and John began moving in that direction.

John didn't know how late it was; the sky had no sign of brightening. He judged it was possibly one or two in the morning. To be sure, he pulled out the compass from his pocket. The compass had a built-in clock. When he shone his flashlight down at it briefly, he was surprised to see that it was almost 5:30am! And yet the sky was mercilessly black in the dark. No expectation of a gray dawn around the canopies of leaves overhead.

The directional compass was spinning out of control, not hesitating for a moment to get a steady sight on a magnetic north. It just spun around crazily like a lazy clock, going counterclockwise.

Something wasn't right.

This place was wrong.

The child's laughter rang out again, this time seeming to echo around him. It was impossible to tell which direction it came. It seemed to bounce around him in waves, getting closer and closer to him.

"Hello!" He called out, this time no longer a greeting but a cry.

Finally, the familiar silence settled in around him again. There was no more echo, just the oppressive smothering of quiet. He turned around to try to find his way back to the cabin when his flashlight picked something up.

A red shirt.

That's what he saw at first.

He slowly raised his flashlight and saw the smiling face of a little boy. Brown-haired and otherwise healthy looking, he stared at John with a big smile.

"Hello!" John said, his voice softening a little bit. He knelt down and slowly approached the boy.

"What's your name?" He asked the boy.

"I'm Sam." He smiled.

"Sam?" John's brain went back, back to the pathetic printouts George brought to him. The first case he told him about. The two brothers fishing. Elliott and Sam.

1965.

Missing since 1965. The date stuck out in John's mind vividly. There was no way...

"Sam, do you have a brother?" He asked, probing.

"Yeah, Elliott. Why?"

John's blood chilled. What in the hell was going on here? Where was he?

Sam giggled at him. Smiled knowingly.

"What, Sam?" He asked, suspicious, cautious. Not entirely sure that he wasn't going crazy.

And a part of him hoped he was. That he was absolutely insane. Because the alternative was just too difficult to grasp.

"You belong to him now." Sam smiled.

"To… to who?" John asked, not wanting to hear the answer.

Sam didn't reply, he just kept smiling. That haunting, ghastly smile that terrified him more than any druggie or murderer he'd ever had the misfortune to cross. He was terrified. And that angered him. He came for a reason. And he was going to get his answers.

"He's a trickster. He pretends to be people he's not. He's smart that way," Sam said, pointing to his head as if to illustrate the point.

Trickster? Was that how he got Helen out here? Pretended to be Jenny? Calling for help?

If that was the reality of what he was dealing with, John thought, he was in big trouble. George believed it may have been powerful beyond comprehension, but not intelligent.

Highly intelligent.

"Sam, is there a woman here? Helen? A woman named Helen?"

Sam, the tainted little boy that he was, merely smiled. Infuriatingly quiet.

Just when John thought he was going to explode, grab the little kid by the neck and make him talk, Sam's face fell. Whatever merriment was there, fake or otherwise, dropped away completely.

"He's coming."

"Who is?" John asked. He looked around as the trees seemed to bend and sway, despite there being no wind.

Where the hell was he?

When he looked back down, Sam was gone. A quick thought emerged in his mind; something George said last night before they fell asleep. About another realm. About a hunting ground for a hungry beast.

But this place... perpetual night. Time didn't seem to exist here. In the time he spent speaking with Sam, his clock remained the same. No time had passed.

Hunting ground.

Is that what this is? A hunting ground for something primitive, something archaic? John didn't want to stick around to find out. He ran back in the darkness, in the direction of the cabin. He hoped that he hadn't wandered so deep that he'd lost his bearings.

His footsteps and the crunching of twigs underfoot were the only sounds he could hear. That would be a comfort in most situations, he thought to himself. But here, he knows whatever this thing is, it moves silently. And it is out there.

He almost cried with relief when his flashlight washed over the front of the cabin.

"George! George, we gotta get out of..." He threw open the cabin door, shined his light down on the ground.

Nothing.

No gear, no backpacks, no sleeping bags, no shotgun.

No George.

"What the..."

That was when he heard the growling.

Deep and low, it started out as a rumble and within a few seconds he could hear it reverberate through the thick trees. John threw himself into the cabin and slammed the door shut, hunkering down low against the door, bracing it.

It was difficult to tell how far off the growl was. Whether it was right behind him or far away.

Yet another trick the woods played on him. No concept of time, no concept of space, no concept of the fundamental rules that governed the natural world.

He pulled his Glock from the holster, flipped off the safety. Looked around the cabin once more.

He couldn't believe George had taken off and left him behind. After everything they went through to figure it out together, to get up there together. After the speech he made about sticking it out, so that John could get the closure he needed. It was all bullshit.

He knew it was a long shot, but he needed to try to see if he could get to where the car was parked. No doubt George was already long gone, but he had to try.

John waited for a while. He wasn't sure if the creature was close to him, just waiting for that door to open before striking. The cabin was merely a small curing cabin, not built with any luxuries at all. Therefore, there were no windows facing the front of the cabin. No way for him to get a quick look before deciding to make a run for it.

There was a small thud outside, right near the door, and then what sounded like heavy footsteps running away.

John waited a moment longer.

"Lord, please grant me strength," he prayed, knowing that his courage was running thin. Steadying his breath, he finally grasped the doorknob in his sweaty palm and turned.

His flashlight shone over the trees and bushes beyond, not seeing anything. His breath continued to plume out in front of him in the cold, though the air felt thick and static.

Now was his moment. Now was the time to move.

He stepped outside of the cabin.

And froze.

Something was on the ground near his feet.

He was terrified.

It was too dark to pick it out, and he had to will himself to be brave enough to aim his flashlight at it.

Sobs already struck his throat, anticipating what it was.

It can't be.

Sweet God, it can't be…

"Lord, please…" He muttered softly, his eyes closing, his face turning up to the dark, uncaring sky.

He knew he needed to leave.

He needed to run.

He had to get out.

The urgency to move struck his skin, his bones, his blood.

Everything pulled him away.

From that moment, that second.

From that thing lying on the ground.

With a deep breath, he aimed the flashlight downward.

Took in a sharp breath.

There, on the ground, ripped cartilage and flesh dangling from the base, blood long since dried....

There, on the ground, was Helen's head.

A crackle from a log in the woodstove popped, and George opened his eyes. The morning sun was streaming through the single window on the back of the cabin behind him. He sat up and rubbed his eyes.

"You awake, John?" He asked and turned his head.

The bed was empty.

Alarmed, George stood. Looked around.

The fire had fallen to embers, still crackling underneath the surface but much cooler. John's sleeping bag was still there, though it was unzipped and open. His pack was still in the corner on the floor where he left it. The Glock was missing.

George grabbed the shotgun by the door and opened it up, stepped out into the early morning sunshine. The woods were empty. Not a sign of John anywhere.

He knelt down to the dirt beneath his feet, felt the grass with his hand. Shut his eyes. Trying to pick up a vibration, a sense of the direction John had gone. Anything.

But it was all dead. No hum, no nothing. It was dead land.

George stood. "John!" He screamed into the woods. It echoed throughout the thick thatch of trees. Came back to him. Died away.

Nothing.

He was out here alone.

Tree branches ripped at him when he ran, blindly, through the forest. The darkness was intrusive, suffocating, but he refused to scream. He didn't want to give the thing any indication of where he was. Even though he could feel it around him. Surrounding him.

Intelligent.

Devious.

Manipulative.

This thing knew exactly where he was. It was toying with him. Giving him crumbs, leaving him a trail.

Only to show him that it was in control.

It held the power.

This was its land.

This was its realm.

He was the intruder here.

Helen. His Helen.

Tears streamed down his face, running, running for the car, for the road. It couldn't be far.

Her head was contorted in a look of fear, frozen and suspended in time. The skin had already begun to wither and rot, to dry and shrink away from the bone.

She had been dead a while.

He wanted to scream. To curse the world.

To sob to the stars that blinked above him, winking at him, taunting him.

Oblivious to the hell that he was running through.

He just kept running. Maneuvering his way through the brush, around the trees, trying to be as quiet as possible, terrified that the thing, whatever it was, was right on his heels.

Yet he knew it was behind him. It was around him.

It was everywhere.

Omnipotent.

Legion.

He saw something looming ahead through the trees. His lungs were on fire. His legs felt like lead. But whatever was up ahead. It had to be the car. George's car.

Maybe he was inside. Waiting for John to arrive.

Maybe he'd gotten too freaked out to stay in the cabin.

Maybe he just couldn't stay in the woods any longer.

Maybe it had become too much for him.

The clearing came into focus.

He stopped dead in his tracks.

Frozen in disbelief.

Ahead of him, through a thicket of trees, was the cabin.

"No!" He cried out, falling to his knees.

It wasn't possible. It's not possible. He thought to himself, trying to rationalize what was happening.

He'd run west through the trees. Only west. How did he wind up here again? It was scientifically, mathematically impossible.

Yet, there on the ground, a few feet away from the door of the cabin, was the severed head.

His wife.

The beautiful blonde hair he would lace his fingers through; the cheeks he would kiss softly when she was sleeping; the lips that curved mischievously when she smiled…

The sobs came. Raw and hard.

He cried loudly to the uncaring darkness around him.

The perpetual dark.

The never-ending night.

That would surround him for the rest of his days.

He no longer cared.

John had to admit to himself, finally, the unknowable truth.

That he finally had his answers.

And he had paid the ultimate price…

EPILOGUE

The door chimed as he walked through, the fluorescent lighting overhead harsh and dramatic. The clerk behind the counter stood, his gaze drifting up and up to the tall man walking up the aisle.

He'd seen him before. Many, many times before.

"George," he greeted, putting down the dog-eared book that he had been reading. His face fell as he threw a glance to the calendar hanging on the wall next to him.

"Shit, is it that time already?" He asked.

George nodded somberly.

Fifteen minutes later, a stack of fresh fliers in his hand, George walked down the sidewalk on Main Street, his eyes searching for the best focal points.

Across the street, he caught Officer Brad Rhodes walking into the station. Rhodes threw him a quick wave, his eyes dark and haunted. George nodded in reply.

He continued along the street, coming to a thick, sturdy light pole. Immediately he went to work. He'd brought a staple gun with him this time; the tape never seemed to hold for very long.

George knew it was a fruitless exercise, yet he knew it was one that he had to continue to do. For his own sanity. For his own fragile, fragile sanity.

Every night, he drove up the familiar road. Straight to the mouth to the woods, where he drove with John. Sat in his car for hours, windows rolled down, just listening.

For what, he didn't know.

Hoping.

Hoping he would stumble out of the woods, bedraggled and dazed but otherwise fine.

Hoping some clue might materialize as to what happened to him.

He was never brave enough to go back in. Could never bring himself to be courageous enough to do so. John was taken without a sound, without a word.

And as much as he wanted to learn the truth, he wasn't willing to risk what he would have to sacrifice to know it.

He finished stapling and took a step back to take it in. With a deep sigh, he moved and began to trudge down the street, looking for another pole.

The fliers were put up every month.

Religiously.

For a full year.

George knew he could never move forward. That he would never be able to come to terms with what happened.

And the owl…

The owl.

He knew now the cards were, yet again, frighteningly accurate.

Never wrong.

He knew now that the owl…

…the owl was for John…

THE END

TWO MILES

ABOUT THE AUTHOR

Angela Darling is a novelist who lives in the Seattle area. Dubbed "The Queen of the Macabre," her novels are richly infused with history, romance and dark gothic horror. Her biggest writing influences include Edgar Allan Poe, V.C. Andrews and Shirley Jackson.

She has been writing for over 30 years, completing her first full-length novel, "War" when she was just 15 years old.

COMING SOON

SAUL: A ROGUE RIVER TALE

www.angela-darling.com

One day, a group of hunters found a strange man standing deep in the Rogue River woods. He was well dressed and silent, offering no clues as to who he was, where he was from, or why he was standing quietly in the middle of the thick forest.

He gave only the name of Saul. Despite persistent prodding by the local Police Chief Don Hartley, he gave no other information.

Then one morning, he spoke. He recited a riddle that no one could decipher. It didn't seem to make any sense; until the news of a plane crash reached Rogue River. And the death toll was exactly what he had predicted.

Over the coming months, he gave warnings of tragic events, things that had not yet come to pass. He predicted the entire town of Rogue River would be wiped out very soon.

And then he disappeared.

The town was left in tatters, trying to comb the woods to find the mysterious Saul, to get answers as to what was to come. It was all up to Police Chief Hartley to decipher this final riddle and rescue his town from imminent doom.

But the real questions remained in the front of Hartley's mind: Who is Saul?

Where did he come from?

Where did he go?

And how could he possibly know what was to happen?